LIBRARY-NEWARK, OHIO 43055
W9-BPP-220

Love in the Mountains

JANET H. BURNHAM

G.K. Hall & Co. • Chivers Press
Thorndike, Maine USA   Bath, England

This Large Print edition is published by Thorndike Press, USA and by Chivers Press, England.

Published in 2000 in the U.S. by arrangement with Janet H. Burnham.

Published in 2000 in the U.K. by arrangement with the author.

U.S. Softcover	0-7838-9227-6	(Paperback Series Edition)
U.K. Hardcover	0-7540-4348-7	(Chivers Large Print)
U.K. Softcover	0-7540-4349-5	(Camden Large Print)

The text of this Large Print edition is unabridged.
Other aspects of the book may vary from the original edition.

Set in 16 pt. Plantin by PerfecType.

Printed in the United States on permanent paper.

British Library Cataloguing-in-Publication Data available

Library of Congress Cataloging-in-Publication Data

Burnham, Janet Hayward.
Love in the mountains / Janet H. Burnham.
p. cm.
ISBN 0-7838-9227-6 (lg. print : sc : alk. paper)
1. Home ownership — Fiction. 2. Love stories — Authorship — Fiction. 3. Vermont — Fiction. 4. Large type books. I. Title.
PS3552.U732415 L68 2000
823′.914—dc21 00-059796

This book is dedicated to George,
Megaera and Fran for years of ears
and patient hearts — and to
Kay Ketcham, my number one fan.

One

It was perfect! Tory stood at the bottom of a rain-soaked field and looked up at the old farmhouse. The trees edging the field were November barren and still dripping from the rain that had only just stopped. Excitement welled up in her. From here it really did look just as she imagined it should. She tried to arrange her face to look impassive before she turned around and headed back to the car where the real estate saleswoman was waiting.

'Well, what do you think?' the woman asked brightly. 'Do you want to take a closer look?'

Tory nodded. 'It's a possibility,' she answered noncommittally, and hoped she wasn't letting any of her excitement show through.

Having her own place in the country in Vermont had been Tory's dream since a ski weekend during her sophomore year in college. She had fallen in love that weekend with the gentle back-home atmosphere of Vermont, and had vowed that one day she would make it her home.

Her work as an illustrator had taken her to New York City, where she lived in squalor, as her friend Andy called it, just so that she could save every possible penny toward this day.

'Any day now I expect to find you living out of shopping-bags on the street,' Andy would say to her and shake her tawny head in disbelief. And spent every last cent to live as elegantly as possible. She was a successful model, and her considerable income allowed her to live in virtual opulence. 'My good friend Tory, the bag-lady illustrator,' she called Tory in exasperation. Tory would just smile indulgently and go right on saving all she could against the day she could make her dream come true.

And now the long-awaited day had arrived. She had what she hoped was enough money to buy her dream. She also had made some very good connections during her years of working in the city. So that now she could continue to illustrate for a number of publishing houses and live wherever she pleased.

She purposely frowned. She mustn't let her enthusiasm jack up the price. She would have been disappointed to know that her sparkling blue eyes gave her away.

The real estate woman, whose name was Lottie Munger, expertly pulled into the yard and parked. Tory rubbed the steam off the window and looked at the friendly old house. Up close it was even better than she had dared hope.

'Mr Caldwell must be out.' Lottie was jiggling a handful of keys.

'Is he the owner?' Tory asked.

'No, the renter,' Lottie answered.

'The house is rented?' Tory asked in surprise.

'Yes,' Lottie nodded. 'The owners would prefer to sell, but while they're waiting for someone to come along and meet their price, they decided to rent.'

Tory's heart sank. The price was probably outrageous. She didn't have the heart to ask the price, just yet. Maybe she wouldn't like the inside, she told herself reasonably, and then it wouldn't matter.

Lottie finally found the right key and opened the door. The scent of freshly baked bread greeted them as they stepped over the threshold.

The house was small and cosy with braided rugs on the floor. Mr Caldwell, whoever he was, had good taste, Tory noted.

And Mr Caldwell, whatever else he was, was handy in the kitchen. Three evenly browned loaves of bread sat on their sides cooling on the kitchen counter. Both women eyed the loaves hungrily. They looked at each other and laughed. 'I suppose Mr Caldwell can count to three,' Tory giggled.

'Yes, I imagine he'd miss one,' Lottie agreed with a grin.

The living-room was strewn with papers and books. A typewriter was set up in one corner, and there were boxes of typing-paper stacked beside it.

'I understand Mr Caldwell is a writer,' Lottie said.

'What does he write?' Tory asked.

'I don't know,' Lottie answered, 'but the village gossip is in favour of scandalous novels,' she grinned mischievously.

At the back of the kitchen there was a large rough room that had been the woodshed. Tory sighed. The time had come to ask the price. She mentally crossed her fingers. If she could have crossed her toes inside her shoes, she would have. 'What are they asking for this place?'

Lottie named a price that was on the high end of the scale of what Tory could afford. It wouldn't leave her much to make any of the repairs she could see were necessary.

'That includes fifty acres of land,' Lottie added, her professional eye seeing Tory wince inwardly. 'It's a good investment.'

'Is that a firm price?' Tory asked.

'I'm afraid so,' Lottie answered. 'Mr Caldwell has made several offers that seemed reasonable, and the owners have said no. They seem to be prepared to wait until someone is willing to pay what they're asking.'

A car door slammed in the yard. 'Someone's here,' Lottie said unnecessarily. They both watched the kitchen door. A curly dark head appeared.

'Hello Ladies!' The voice was deep and masculine. 'Mrs Munger, isn't it?' he smiled. 'Showing my house?'

Tory noted that the appearance of this handsome dark-haired man made Lottie Munger just the smallest amount flustered. Lottie introduced them and giggled in the process.

Mitchell Caldwell graciously shook Tory's hand. He wasn't at all what Tory had pictured. She had been thinking in terms of short, small-boned serious professor-type, someone who wrote textbooks and could bake bread too.

'Well,' said Mitchell Caldwell in his rich full voice that for some reason made Tory's insides shiver, 'what do you think of my little house? Or should I say,' he corrected himself, 'my little rented house?'

'It's very cosy,' Tory answered with a smile, and she looked at her hand to see what had caused the small twinge she had felt when Mitchell shook it.

'Something wrong?' He had seen the puzzled look on her face.

'Oh no,' she was quick to reply.

'Miss Higgins is an illustrator from New York,' Lottie joined the conversation. 'She's looking for a house in the country.'

'I see,' he answered. 'A weekend retreat?' he asked. His amber eyes were serious.

'No,' replied Tory. 'I plan to live here . . . or wherever or whatever I purchase.' She was still anxious not to seem too interested.

'Well, if you do decide to buy this place, you will have made a good choice. It's got all the solitude and quiet you'll need to work. Plus beautiful views out every window to feed the artist's soul.' He ran a hand through his thick wavy hair. 'Now, just listen to me. I don't know why I'm trying to sell you on this place. I'd like to buy it myself.'

Both women smiled indulgently at his guileless gesture.

'Then why don't you buy it?' Tory asked, curious to know why he hadn't offered the owners what they wanted. Maybe he knew it wasn't worth the asking price.

'Can't afford to,' he answered. 'Divorces don't come cheaply,' he added darkly.

Tory sensed the anger and bitterness in those few words.

Mitchell gave Tory a piercing look, and Tory felt momentarily like a butterfly impaled in a collection. There was something unnerving about this man. Tory, who was usually so sure of herself, was only too aware that she hadn't felt quite so shaky around a man since Adam. She squared her shoulders. She didn't have to worry about Mitchell Caldwell. If she bought this house, he'd have to move out. And she'd never see him again. And as far as Adam was concerned, she didn't have to think about him either. That was over and done with. A closed chapter in her life. And good riddance.

Mitchell excused himself to unload his groceries.

Lottie and Tory walked back through the house to talk of money and houses and possibilities. The more they talked, the more certain Tory became that she wanted this house. Before they re-entered the kitchen, Tory had said she'd take it.

Mitchell was just putting the last of his groceries away. 'Come to any decision?' He began pulling on some stubborn plastic wrap, preparing to wrap his bread.

'Miss Higgins has decided to take it,' Lottie began brightly but ended with some hesitancy.

'Oh?' The plastic wrap paused in mid-air. Tory wondered if his demeanour would change, having the house sold out from under him, so to speak. 'I knew I shouldn't have made this bread,' he said seriously.

Both women raised their eyebrows in question. It wasn't exactly the response they were expecting.

'The aroma of fresh bread always sells a house,' Mitchell explained, a slight smile curling up the corners of his mouth. 'Do you bake bread, Miss Higgins?'

Tory didn't know if he was intending to poke fun at her or not. 'No,' she answered tentatively. 'But I intend to learn. It goes with the territory, doesn't it?'

'Seems to,' he answered, as he deftly wrapped his loaves. 'It's all in the kneading . . . in the hands.' He raised his palms towards her to illustrate. Such large hands you have grandfather, Tory thought to herself. The better NOT to grab me with, she also told herself.

Mitchell unaccountably winked at her. Tory had the odd sensation that he had just read her mind.

He saw them to the door and put one of the loaves of still warm bread in Tory's hand. 'Here, owner. Your first house-warming present. Congratulations!'

Tory could feel the intensity of those amber eyes following her all the way to the car. He stood in the doorway and watched them drive down the hill.

Tory put the loaf of bread on her lap. Its warmth seeped through her wool skirt and warmed her thighs. She had the momentary feeling of large warm hands on her thighs. She put the loaf of bread on the car seat. So much for large warm hands on my thighs, she thought to herself.

The closing on the house went without a hitch. The following day it snowed just enough to make the ground look as though it had been sprinkled with powdered sugar.

Mitchell moved out. She didn't see him go. One day he was there, and the next he wasn't. Somewhere way back in her mind a little sting of having lost something pricked her consciousness. She dismissed it.

The moving-van arrived and unloaded Tory's furniture. The kindly old man who was in charge of the crew kept asking her questions. He just couldn't understand why a pretty young thing would want to live in the country — by herself.

'You ought to stay in the city, Missy, where there's plenty of young fellows. You need a husband and children. This is no kind of life for a young woman.' He shook his head at all her reasons. Tory finally gave up trying to convince him that she hadn't lost her mind. She didn't tell him that part of her original dream had been to move to Vermont with a husband named Adam. She didn't tell him that dreams sometimes do not work out the way you plan.

The moving-men were finished in the early afternoon. Tory thanked them, shut the door, and spun around in the middle of the floor with her arms outstretched. 'Mine, all mine,' she grinned happily.

She spent the rest of the day trying to bring some sense of order out of the chaos of her belongings.

Two

At five o'clock it was almost dark. Tory was thinking about looking for some cheese and biscuits, when there was a knock on the door. On her way to answer the knock, she glanced at herself in the mirror she had hung earlier. 'Ugh!' she said to her reflection. Her fine blond hair was escaping at the sides of the kerchief she had tied around her head. And there was a large smudge of black on her cheek which probably had come from the wood stove in the living-room. 'Anyone who comes here on moving-day will just have to take me as I am,' she muttered to herself.

A smiling Mitchell Caldwell was standing on the doorstep. 'You look like something out of a fairy tale . . . Cinderella, I think.' His amber eyes grinned.

'And who are you?' she grinned in return. 'Prince Charming or one of the Seven Dwarfs?'

'Come to think about it, even though you flatter me by suggesting I might be Prince

Charming, I'm probably Grumpy.' He turned down the edges of his mouth and scowled.

'Grumpy, is it? What's wrong? Did you forget something?'

'I don't think so.' He swung around a large picnic basket that he had been holding behind his back. 'I've got fried chicken, potato salad, tossed salad, fresh bread, fruit and *voilà!*' He pulled out a bottle of champagne. 'To toast your new home! I even brought knives and forks and plates, in case you can't lay hands on yours.' Without waiting to be invited, he walked into the kitchen and began clearing a space on the table to put down his basket.

Tory still stood at the open door watching him in complete surprise. 'Shut the door, Cinderella. You're letting your heat out. And speaking of heat,' he was busily emptying his basket of goodies, 'have you had any trouble with your furnace yet?'

Tory shut the door and answered no.

'You will,' he replied.

'Oh? What's wrong with my furnace?' she asked. She was beginning to chafe at his high-handed ways.

'It's old and tired. There's nothing wrong that a new one wouldn't fix.'

'A n . . . n . . . new one?' she stammered. 'Are you sure?'

He turned and stood with one hand on a slim hip. 'I lived with the beast in your basement for two years. It required a lot of attention. You have to jiggle its widget and poke its buttons.' He grinned at her.

His eyes, she noted, weren't only on her face as he spoke, but were taking calculated stock of her whole figure. She wondered in spite of herself if he was finding the picture suitable. She walked behind the kitchen island counter to cut off some of his view.

He was very aware that his gaze was making her uncomfortable. And worst of all, he seemed to be enjoying her uneasiness. 'Come on over here, Cinderella, and let us break bread together.' He cleared off a chair for her. 'I'll show you how to placate the beast after we've eaten.'

She had half a mind to throw him and his food out the door. But she was tired and the food did look wonderful. She sat down, telling herself one more sarcastic remark and out he goes. Just as she suspected, the food was delicious. And Caldwell, she was pleased to find, could be the perfect gentleman, when he wanted to be.

'Where are you living now?' she asked by way of conversation.

'In the village,' he answered between bites of chicken. 'It's not bad, but there are a lot of distractions in a household of little children.'

'Little children?' Somehow she couldn't picture him with children under foot.

'I have my own room and bath, but I have to share the kitchen with the owners and their two rug rats, ages two and four.' He sighed. 'It's not the ideal arrangement for an old grouch like me.

I have a hard time working when there are wails of childish delight and baby gibberish coming from the other side of my walls at all hours of the day and night. I'm looking for something else.'

For some reason the picture of Mitchell Caldwell dealing with two- and four-year-olds made her smile.

They lingered over the champagne, chatting easily. Tory was beginning to feel at ease with Caldwell. He was easy to know, and he listened.

They cleaned up the crumbs and packed the leftovers back in the picnic basket. Then, they adjourned to the basement, as Mitchell put it. He carefully showed Tory all the widgets and wires, and told her when to push which button. 'Got that?' He turned those serious amber eyes on her frowning face.

'I think so,' she answered, mentally noting that dream houses came with malfunctioning furnaces. Having lived in apartments all her life, she had never given furnaces a thought. 'What's that contraption?' She pointed to a silver tank in the corner.

'That, my dear homeowner, is your water-tank. And the other,' he pointed to a black tank, 'is your oil-tank.'

'What do I do with those?'

Mitchell gave her a surprised look. 'You've never lived in a house before, have you?'

She shook her head no. She was beginning to feel as if she had just been transported to a strange planet, where all the workings were different.

‘A babe in the woods,’ he grinned at her.

‘I’m a fast learner,’ she answered in her own defence. ‘Don’t play a superior male chauvinist with me, thank you.’

‘I wouldn’t dream of it,’ he answered. Tory heard the hint of sarcasm in his voice, but she wisely chose to ignore it. Right now, there was a lot of information he had that she needed to know. If he needed throwing out, she could do it later.

Mitchell carefully explained all the systems in the house and told her how to cope with each one’s eccentricities. Finally he ran a hand through his hair. ‘There, I think I’ve covered everything you’ll need to know for a while.’ He glanced at his watch. ‘It’s getting late. You’ve had a long day. Time I was leaving. I might turn into a pumpkin if I stay too long at the ball.’

Tory smiled at his wit and thanked him for the picnic supper and for all his information. She put out a hand to shake his. He took her slim hand in his large one and gently raised it to his lips. ‘My pleasure, madame.’ He bowed and turned to go.

Tory wondered why it was his touch set off little explosions of excitement in her. What had happened to her usual armour against such male advances? Must be the champagne, she decided.

Mitchell had picnic basket in hand and had just reached out to open the door, when he stopped. ‘Hey, I just had a crazy idea!’ He turned to face her again. ‘Promise me you won’t say no until you’ve heard me out.’

Tory was taken off guard. She nodded her head almost automatically.

'Look, you need a caretaker and I need a place of peace and quiet to work . . .'

'Absolutely not.' She could see immediately what he was going to suggest.

'Wait,' he commanded, 'you haven't heard what I have in mind.'

'I've heard enough to know the answer is no,' she answered primly.

'You promised to hear me out,' he reminded her. 'Or do you work on the old-fashioned female principle that a woman can change her mind. That's just a poor excuse for not keeping your word, you know. You women . . .' He stopped in mid-sentence and changed course. Tory knew he meant to say — 'You women are all alike,' but then thought better of it.

'Please listen.'

'All right, I'll listen.' She crossed her arms.

'I really do need to find a place where I can work on my novel. Yesterday I wrote a total of three sentences. At that rate I'll finish my book at age 92.'

'That's not my problem,' Tory answered.

'You're right, it's not. Your problem will be dealing with all the old systems in the house. Don't forget I lived here for two years. I know what you're up against. So, unless you've got money enough to replace the plumbing, heating and wiring, you're going to have trouble.'

'There are such things as plumbers and electricians in the wilds of Vermont, I take it,' Tory replied crisply.

'Yes, of course,' he countered. 'But they're expensive too. Look, I could throw some insulation up out in the woodshed and make it pretty tight. It wouldn't make a bad room. I'd only need to have an hour or so a day to use the bathroom and the kitchen. You wouldn't even know I was here. I can pay rent and be available any time something goes haywire. I'd only be needing the space for the winter until my book is done. By spring you'll have learned all the ropes, and saved a fair amount of my rent money to begin replacing the worst problems.' He could see she was listening. He pressed on. 'Don't make up your mind right now. Think about it. I'll call you day after tomorrow. It could be a good solution for both of us.'

Fresh from the basement systems lecture, Tory could see that Mitchell's idea in one way wouldn't be a bad one. But the idea of having that enticing hunk of maleness living in her woodshed, rubbing elbows with him every day, was more than she wanted to cope with. She had had enough of strong-willed, opinionated males in Adam. Enough to last a lifetime, thank you.

'At least say you'll think about it.' He ended his spiel with such a heartfelt smile that Tory didn't have courage to say an outright no. Instead she told him: 'I'll think about it . . . but don't count on it.'

'Good,' he replied. He opened the door and bounded off the stoep into the night.

You wouldn't be in such high spirits if you knew my answer, she thought. She watched his car lights disappear down the driveway hill.

She awoke the next morning to sun streaming in her bedroom window. She stuck her nose out from under the old down comforter that had once belonged to her favourite aunt. The room was cold. The 'beast in the basement', as Mitchell had called it, must have gone off during the night. She threw on her clothes as quickly as she could.

Down in the basement the beastly furnace sat there cold and silent. She turned the widget and poked the button, as Mitchell had shown her. The beast roared into action. She backed away and wondered if furnaces ever blew up. The beast rumbled on, like some prehistoric dinosaur grudgingly prodded back to life. Not knowing if she should do anything else, she went back upstairs to brew some coffee.

I'll build a fire in the living-room stove, she said to herself. That will warm things up. She carefully laid newspapers and kindling in the stove and lit it. It crackled cheerfully. In a few moments the room began to fill up with smoke.

Tory had visions of her house going up in flames. She stood momentarily rooted to the spot. Should she throw water on it? Then she remembered, she hadn't opened the damper on the flue. With the damper closed, the smoke had no place to go. She squinced her eyes shut against the smoke, turned the handle on the damper and waited. Thankfully, the smoke stopped pouring into the room. But the room was still full of smoke, so she opened the windows to clear it. 'Off to a bang-up start,' she said out loud. Wouldn't Mitchell Caldwell be laughing at her now.

She listened. The beast was still rumbling in the basement. Good. That at least was working for the moment.

By the time she had made some breakfast, the house was cosy and warm. There, she congratulated herself, that wasn't so bad. I can handle it. So much for Mr Caldwell's idea.

Another hour passed. She was still unwrapping boxes, when she noticed the house getting cold. The fire in the stove had gone out, and the beast was silent again. She turned the widget and punched the button. Nothing happened. She tried it three times with no success. She waited a few minutes and tried it again. Still nothing. Not knowing what else to do, she came back upstairs and called the nearest plumber.

Several hours went by. She had a good fire going in the living-room stove by the time the plumber arrived. It didn't take him long to coax the beast back on. He came upstairs wiping his oily hands on a rag, shaking his head. 'You need a new furnace. I've told Mr Caldwell that for two years. You married to Caldwell?'

Tory was taken aback by the question. 'No, I'm not married to Mr Caldwell,' she answered coldly.

'Oh. Just visiting then?' He smiled a lecherous smile at her.

'No, I'm not visiting,' she shot back. 'This is my house. I bought it,' she added unnecessarily. 'For your information Mr Caldwell no longer lives here.' There, that should fix his nasty curiosity.

'That's too bad,' he answered, still smiling, not at all affected by her answers or her anger. 'Caldwell knew how to toggle up all these old systems. You know anything about plumbing and heating?'

'I don't see that that's any of your business,' she shot back.

He shrugged. 'Just askin', that's all. I meant no harm.'

Tory glared at him.

He didn't seem to notice. He took a stubby pencil from behind his ear, wet the point, and prepared to write on a greasy pad. 'I'll need your name so's my wife can send you a bill.'

If there had been some way to shove him out the door without touching him, Tory would have.

He waited with pencil poised, evidently enjoying the fact that he had rattled her.

'Tory Higgins,' she said through clenched teeth.

'Tory?' He didn't write it.

'Victoria.' She wanted to wring his dirty scrawny neck.

This time he scribbled on his pad, then held the pad at arm's length to scrutinise his handiwork. 'Tory, huh? Never met a Tory before.' He grinned at her. 'Guess we'll be seeing a lot of each other, Tory.'

She winced at the sound of her name in his mouth. Not if I can help it, she wanted to reply. Instead she thanked him for coming and saw him to the door. She silently promised herself never to call him again. Surely there were other plumbers.

The beast kept the house warm all the rest of the day, and Tory thanked her lucky stars. But the following morning it was off again. And no amount of button-pushing or widget-twisting could persuade it to come on. She called the only other plumber in the book. He was jammed and wouldn't be able to come until tomorrow. He suggested she call the fellow who had come yesterday, adding that he was much closer. She pleaded with him. He said he'd do the best he could, but he couldn't make any promises. Now that the weather had turned colder, it seemed as if everyone needed him. And old customers came first.

Tory hung up almost in tears. She got out her depleted bank book to check the balance. There was no way she could afford to buy a new furnace right now. She supposed she could take out a loan . . . if she could get one. Her line of work paid fairly well, but it wasn't a steady income that you could count on from month to month to make payments. She preferred to save for whatever she needed.

By the time Mitchell called, she had made up her mind to accept his offer. 'I figured you would,' he answered.

'What do you mean by that?' she asked sharply.

'Down girl,' he replied. 'I only meant that I had lived there. Remember? I know the problems.'

'There will be house rules you'll have to agree to,' she went on.

'Of course,' he answered good-naturedly. 'That's fine. That way we'll both know exactly what's expected, and where we stand.'

Tory bit her lip. 'I don't want to begin our relationship . . . I mean, our business relationship, asking you for a favour, but I find I must. Could you come out now and fix the beast? I can't get the damn thing to work.'

He stayed just long enough to coax the beast back to life and to tell her that he'd be moving in tomorrow . . . if that was all right. Feeling the first bit of warmth seep back into the house, Tory felt it was more than all right. She didn't need a man, of that she was certain. But she had to admit the beast in the basement certainly needed a keeper.

Three

Tory dreamed of Adam that night. Adam her almost husband. Adam, who had been so much a part of her life for four years. Adam, who had been so much a part of her very bones and body, that when he left, she was surprised to find she was still she, that there was still a reflection of Tory in the mirror. She had wrapped her life and all her dreams around Adam. They had planned this move to Vermont together. Had saved for it. It was their own special private dream.

And then Adam had told her that fateful day that he was taking a job in California. Right out of the blue. Just told her, as though he were talking about buying broccoli. They had just made love, and Tory was still floating in the sweet aftermath of passions released. Adam had his head propped up in one hand, the other was transcribing gentle circles on her breast. Their love-making had always been fiery and passionate. Tory had felt that it was perfect. She would listen to some of her friends' long sad tales of unfulfilled love-making, and feel extremely lucky, even smug, in the knowledge that she and Adam had none of those problems.

Adam had bent over her breast and nibbled on her aroused nipple. That was when he told her. He couldn't have chosen a worse time.

Adam was a master of the wrong moment, that was how she thought of it at first, that was some part of the excuse she made for him. When she got to the point of stripping away all the bangles and a stage-dressing she herself had hung on the man, she could finally see him for what he was. He was a supremely selfish man. Handsome, sexy, suave. He was all those things too, but they only served to hide the true Adam. When her eyes were at last looking clearly, she knew that at bottom he was very self-centred, and yes, even cruel.

Since Adam had departed over a year ago, she had made up her mind that she would never again be so taken in by a man. Obviously, she had a problem too. If she could think Adam was so perfect for four long years, what other things could she be foolish enough to believe? She had dated some, but nothing ever came of it except some lukewarm friendships. Tory was very careful.

In the dream Adam had been chasing her. Part of her wanted to stop and feel again his hands on her body. Her legs ached to be spread, to welcome the weight of his body on hers. But she knew to stop running would also mean the end of herself. She would no longer be Tory if she stopped and let him catch her.

She woke in a cold sweat, tears of anger and frustration dampening her pillow. It was two in the morning. Silvery moonlight was streaming in the window, making puddles of ghostly light on the polished pine floor. She got up and put on her robe. The house was warm. She sent a silent prayer of thanks to the temperamental beast in the basement. She pulled a chair to the window and sat for a very long time, looking at the bright moonlit landscape, trying to rid her mind of the memories that haunted it.

It was almost morning before she crept back to bed.

She awoke with a start. It was still dark outside. The moon had set. She rubbed her sleepy eyes. Something had awakened her. She peered at the faint lighted face of the alarm clock. Six o'clock. The noise started again. It was hammering. It couldn't be Caldwell, could it? Nobody in their right mind would be doing carpentry work before the sun came up.

She threw on her robe, and felt around on the floor for her slippers. She pulled the sash of her robe tightly around her slim waist and knotted it. 'I'm going to give that man a piece of my mind,' she muttered.

The sound of hammering increased as she approached the woodshed. She threw open the door and was surprised to find the woodshed room full of great rolls of something that looked like pink candy floss.

Mitchell Caldwell turned his head and grinned at her from his perch on the top of the ladder. 'Good morning, landlady.'

'What are you doing?' she demanded. She wasn't going to be taken in by that boyish grin of his.

'Feathering my nest,' he answered still grinning at her, his eyes appreciating the figure beneath her flimsy gown and robe.

'It's a little early, isn't it?' Her voice was hard and all business.

'Not for a Vermonter,' he answered. 'I've already milked the cows.' He was obviously enjoying baiting her.

'I haven't any cows, Mr Caldwell, and what is all this?' She pointed to the giant rolls of pink stuffing.

'That's insulation, my dear landlady. That's what's going to keep me from freezing to death out here. You wouldn't want your boarder to freeze up on you, now would you?'

'Couldn't you wait until daylight before you began? You woke me up!'

'I'm sorry.' He climbed down the ladder, and tried to look contrite. 'There's so much to be done out here, I thought I'd get an early start. And speaking of what's to be done,' he didn't give her a chance to continue spluttering. 'I think we should put in a new electrical entry-box. I have to run new wires out here before I cover it up with insulation. If you can afford to put in a breaker-box, I'll pay for the wire.'

Tory had no idea what he was talking about. And what did he mean by 'we'? It was her house, not his.

Mitchell could see that she was confused. 'See this old wiring?' He pointed to two wires that ran overhead to the bare bulb that hung in the middle of the room. 'That's old knob-and-tubing wiring. It's brittle and not very safe. All the wiring in the house runs to a fusebox in the basement, where the main line comes in from outside. Fuses also aren't very safe. It would be a good idea to put in a new box with circuit-breakers. I have to run new wiring out here, and I just thought, while I was about it, that I should change the fusebox to a breaker-box — with your permission, that is.'

At least, Tory noted, he did seem to be getting the idea that this was her house. 'Is that very expensive?' she asked.

'A couple of hundred ought to cover it,' he answered.

'A couple of hundred!' What did he think, that she was made of money? Her poor bank book was gasping for breath as it was.

He shrugged. 'It's entirely up to you. I just thought you'd want to do things right.'

Oh, he was infuriating. Of course she wanted to do things right, but she wanted to eat too. She mentally made some calculations. She guessed she could afford a breaker-box, especially since it was a matter of safety. 'All right, put in a breaker-box,' she sighed. 'But please try to be more quiet. I didn't get much sleep last night.'

'Sorry to hear that,' he answered. 'But I'm sorry to tell you, I've never learned to hammer quietly.' With that, he began hammering up lengths of the pink insulation.

Tory slammed the door. The nerve of the man. This arrangement was a bad idea. If only she had enough money to buy a furnace. She climbed back in bed. She lay rigidly with her eyes squeezed shut, willing sleep to return. The hammering continued. She turned her head and felt the dampness of her tears still on the pillow. She flipped it over. Damn men. She pounded the pillow with a fist. This wasn't getting her anywhere. She might as well get up and see if she could find her boxes of art materials. The sooner she set up shop, the sooner she could get some illustrations done. And the sooner she got paid, the sooner she could afford to buy furnaces and breaker-boxes. And the sooner she could have her house all to herself.

Grimly determined, she got up and got dressed.

The steady whack whack whack of the hammer continued, but Tory was so engrossed in opening her boxes that she didn't hear it until it stopped. I wonder what Mr Smart Remark is doing now? Probably thinking up new ways to spend my money, she decided. The door from the woodshed banged shut. Then she heard whistling in the kitchen — her kitchen!

Tory was adjusting her drawing-table in the living-room, when Mitchell appeared in the doorway. He leaned nonchalantly against the door jamb, coffee cup in hand. 'I helped myself to some of your coffee,' he raised the coffee cup, 'hope you don't mind.'

'Hmmmmm,' she answered noncommittally. She did mind, but she could see no way to say so gracefully. She thought if she ignored him, he'd go back to work and leave her alone. But he didn't seem to be in any hurry. Should she tell him to get out of her part of the house? What right did he have to wander around as though he owned the place anyway? A wave of panic swept through her. Why did he have to look so at home standing there like that? Why couldn't he be short and fat and funny-looking? And why did her pulse have to beat a little faster every time he appeared?

'I was wondering about breakfast,' he sipped his coffee — HER coffee — and looked an easy smile in her direction.

She turned and put her hands on her hips. What was this? Did he expect her to make him breakfast? This was too much, very much too much. Furnace or no furnace, she would tell him to go.

Before she could get the words arranged in her mouth, he went on: 'I thought since you're so anxious to get your studio set up, I'd offer to make breakfast.'

She looked at him dumbfounded. Adam never made breakfast. That was her job. He had made it very clear. Cooking was for women. But this wasn't Adam, she reminded herself. This was an entirely different person, who even knew how to make bread. He was probably handier in the kitchen than she was, she reflected unhappily.

'Thank you, Mr Caldwell, that's very kind of you. But I'll make my own.'

'Just thought I'd offer,' he shrugged. 'Sure you won't change your mind.'

'I'm sure.' She pretended to be very busy with the contents of a large box of drawing-tablets.

She could hear him whistling in the kitchen. The smell of bacon frying made her stomach grumble. She waited until she could stand it no longer, then she headed for the kitchen.

She poured herself a glass of orange juice and popped two pieces of bread in the toaster.

Mitchell was sprawled out at the table, his empty plate before him, seemingly totally engrossed in reading the paper.

Tory was annoyed. She didn't want him bothering her; yet, she didn't like it when he ignored her either.

She plunked her plate on the table with a thud.

Mitchell put down the paper and looked at her. 'Yes?' He couldn't help smiling.

Tory was even more annoyed. 'Everyone must pick up after him or herself,' she announced severely. 'Rules of the house.' She eyed the greasy frying-pan.

'Yes, of course,' Mitchell answered good-naturedly.

'You may use the bottom shelf in the refrigerator,' she went on in her schoolteacher voice.

'That's fine,' he nodded.

'And you can have the top and bottom cupboards next to the door for your kitchen equipment and groceries.'

He just nodded his head, the slight smile still on his lips.

Tory looked at the dark curly hair on his arms, where his light blue shirt was rolled back. They were such sturdy arms and hands. She could feel the familiar ache in her thighs begin. She looked away. That was dangerous, so very dangerous. She mustn't let the look of him get to her. He was just an ordinary man. Nobody special. This was just a business arrangement, nothing more.

'Is that all you have for breakfast?' he asked.

'My breakfast is no business of yours, I don't believe, Mr Caldwell.'

He studied her for a moment before he answered. 'You're absolutely correct, Miss Higgins. It's no business of mine.' He smiled again. The amber eyes were flecked with green. I've noticed that because I'm an artist, she told herself. Not because of anything else.

'But while we are touching on what might be business of mine,' he went on. 'I was wondering if you might want to rewire the kitchen?'

'Rewire the kitchen!' she shrieked. 'Just take care of your part of the house, and leave mine alone!'

She shook her finger at him. 'Don't get carried away with your breaker-boxes, and knobs and tubes and . . . and . . .' she spluttered into silence.

He had straightened up in his chair, and had folded the newspaper. He was watching her performance with the same half-smile. Damn him. Damn his damn smile, Tory thought furiously.

'Calm down,' he said soothingly. 'I forgot you're a city gal with no knowledge of elderly houses in need of repair. I'm not trying to bankrupt you, if that's what you're worried about. It just occurred to me that it might be a good idea to do the kitchen wiring too. Most of it runs up the wall here between the woodshed and the kitchen. If I go ahead and put up the insulation, you'll have to tear it out at some later date to do the wires. It could save you a lot of time and trouble, not to mention money, to do it now.'

Why did he have to be so maddeningly logical? And why did he have to know all sorts of good reasons she should spend her precious little horde of money? She shut her eyes. 'How much?'

'A couple of hundred,' he answered.

'You've already spent a couple of hundred on me, and the morning isn't even over. What will it be this afternoon? I'll be bankrupt before the day is over.'

'You do get riled, don't you?' His mouth had quit smiling, but his eyes still held a hint of it. It hadn't disappeared altogether. 'I had a suggestion on how we could handle this . . . if you're through?'

Oh, he was maddening. Tory gritted her teeth and took a deep breath. 'Go on,' she answered with steely control.

'I would be willing to buy the wire for the kitchen, if you'd be willing to count it as my first month's rent. I think I should remind you, that all my labour is free. If you had to hire someone to do all the renovating I'm doing, it would cost you two to three thousand dollars in labour alone.' He paused. 'Well, what do you think?'

Tory didn't know what to think. For the life of her she couldn't poke a hole in his reasoning. She knew nothing about wires and houses. It all seemed perfectly logical and made good sense. Then why was she so agitated? It was the man himself. He was hard to take. So superior. So sure of himself. So damned enticing.

'Well?' he asked again.

'Let me think about it,' she answered. She put another slice of bread in the toaster and promptly blew a fuse. She shook her head in disbelief. 'Okay, okay, I'm convinced. Call off your gremlins. It's a deal.'

Four

The rest of the day went without a hitch.

Mitchell disappeared into the woodshed, and all Tory heard of him was the steady hammering of his ongoing renovation work. She could imagine those nicely muscled arms swinging in rhythm. Stop it. Don't think that, she told herself severely.

They each had lunch, but at different times. The only trace she saw of him was the neatly rewrapped luncheon meat on the bottom shelf of the refrigerator.

Well, maybe this crazy living-arrangement is going to work after all, she thought. She was well aware that there was something about the man that increased her pulse-rate. She would just ignore it, that's all. Just because he was handsome and lived in her house, she would not let passion rule the day . . . or night, she smirked. As long as he stuck to the woodshed, and she didn't have to see him, she could live with that for a little while. It would be easy.

Spring was only around the corner.

Dusk came early, and with it, the snow that had been threatening all day. Tory kept turning on the outside light to watch the big spidery flakes fill up the yard. Her yard. Her fifty acres. How incredible it seemed that she, Tory Higgins, owned fifty acres of dirt and rocks and grass and trees. She had never owned anything that you couldn't pick up and carry away. To own fifty acres of land attached securely to the state of Vermont, was a marvellous dream come true.

She went to bed dreaming of a soft white world. There were no dreams that frightened her. The house was warm. She smiled in her sleep.

The next morning the house was bone cold. Even under Aunt Marian's down comforter, Tory shivered. The furnace must have gone off hours ago. Why hadn't Caldwell fixed it? Some keeper of the beast he was. If he wasn't going to be more responsible than this, then out he goes!

Tory put on her robe and then wrapped an afghan around her shoulders. Her flimsy night clothes were little protection against the cold. These aren't made for Vermont winters, she thought ruefully. When I can afford it . . . that is, when I'm not buying breakers and boxes and wires . . . I'll get some nice flannel gowns and a wool robe.

She knocked on the woodshed door, but then didn't wait for an answer. It was even colder in the woodshed. A rumpled sleeping-bag was in one corner, covered with several layers of blankets. 'Caldwell?' No answer. She stepped closer to the pile. 'Caldwell?' Still no answer. Tory had a sudden fear that Mitchell Caldwell had frozen to death. She reached out a frightened hand to touch the blankets, when a hearty male voice greeted her from the doorway. 'Good morning, landlady!' She whirled around to see Mitchell Caldwell grinning at her. 'Were you planning to join me? I see you brought your own blanket.' He was eyeing her outfit with obvious relish.

Tory pulled the afghan around her shivering frame. The nerve of him! 'I knocked and there was no answer.' She was suddenly aware that she was trespassing on his territory. 'I wanted you to fix the furnace. Why did you leave it off so long? It's ungodly cold in here!'

'Oh, aren't we touchy this morning. Tsk, tsk, tsk. For your information, my scantily clad landlady, the woodshed isn't heated. There's no way for me to know that the furnace is off until I enter your part of the house. I just got up myself, and was on my way to the basement, when I heard you call my name.'

'Oh,' Tory frowned and bit her lip. He always had an answer. Why did she always have to be wrong? 'If there's no heat out here, how do you expect to keep from freezing?'

'I'm going to put in a wood stove, right over there.' He pointed to a corner. 'If that's all right with you, of course.'

Tory gritted her teeth and shivered.

'Come on, let's go do battle with the beast before you freeze to death in your Florida underwear.'

Florida underwear indeed! Tory didn't budge. He couldn't tell her what to do.

As though he had read her mind, he added: 'I think it's a good idea for you to learn about the furnace. After all, I'm not planning on being here twenty-four hours of every day all winter long.'

Tory reluctantly followed Caldwell to the basement. Of course he was right . . . again. Damn him. And then she couldn't help wondering where he was planning to go and who he might be going with. She pulled the afghan more closely around her slim cold body. It was no business of hers. And she didn't care, really she didn't.

Caldwell was crouched down in front of the cranky old furnace. 'See that opening there?' He had slid back a small metal plate. Tory leaned closer to get a better look. 'Press this down right here . . .' The furnace started with an explosive roar. Acrid smoke billowed out. Mitchell jumped backwards and knocked into Tory, who had been leaning over his shoulder. Tory lost her footing and would have fallen if Mitchell hadn't grabbed her.

'My God! What happened?' Tory leaned into Mitchell's safe strong arms.

'Backfire.' Mitchell held her close.

'Backfire? I thought only cars backfired.'

'No, furnaces can backfire too. Too much fuel

seeped into the starting mechanism.' He was soothing her hair with one hand. The other was holding her securely. She didn't move.

The furnace was rumbling away as though nothing had happened.

Mitchell put a gentle thumb under Tory's chin and tilted her head back so that she had to look straight into his golden eyes. 'Tory?' She knew what he was asking, and she knew her eyes were giving him the answer.

Their lips met and Tory felt that she had stretched across a mighty gulf to reach him. Soft lips on soft lips became more insistent. Tory felt his tongue gently tracing her lips, wanting and waiting for her to open further, to let him in. He kissed the tip of her nose. 'I've wanted to do this since the first day I saw you standing in the kitchen.' His lips slid down her cheek to nibble on an ear-lobe. 'You've wanted me too, haven't you,' he whispered in her ear, his voice husky with passion. It wasn't a question.

'Let's go upstairs where we can be more comfortable.' He led her by the hand, and she followed, her body aflame with needs and wants that she thought she would never feel again. She had thought she had banished such feelings from her life after Adam left. But suddenly, here she was about to make love to a man she hardly knew. Ready and willing to follow him any place that he would lead her.

Mitchell softly closed the basement door behind them. Tory felt she was walking on clouds, surely her feet weren't touching the old pine floors. They were both silent, so quiet. They moved through the air, hardly disturbing it, neither wanting to break the spell.

When they reached Tory's room, Mitchell turned and looked directly into her eyes. His eyes were wide and soft with the depth of his need. He gently squeezed her hand then dropped it, so that they both could undress.

Tory slipped out of her night clothes and Mitchell caught his breath. He slowly shook his head from side to side, admiration plainly glowing on his face. He rushed to remove the last of his clothes. Tory couldn't bear to tear her eyes away from his fine muscular body, with his proud thrusting manhood.

Mitchell pulled back the blankets and Tory crawled between the cold sheets. She shivered, more in expectation than from the cold. She had ceased to feel the coldness of the air. Mitchell climbed in beside her and pulled her pulsing body close to his. Shiver after shiver rippled through her body. 'Your skin is so soft,' he murmured in her ear. 'Like silk — like down.'

The radiators began to tick, as the hot water from the furnace reached them. Mitchell cupped first one breast and then the other. He gently nibbled on each erect nipple, sending waves of need to Tory's aching thighs.

Tory ran her fingers through the curling dark hair on his chest. Her fingers traced circles and figure of eights lower and lower. 'Oh, you tease me so,' he moaned. She slowly approached the seat of his manhood. The feel of him was exquisite, delicious. Tory was beside herself with enjoyment. Every fibre of her body called out to be joined with this strong and gentle man beside her.

The phone beside the bed rang loud and harshly, shattering the fragile bubble of passion that they had so carefully built. They both stopped and held their breath, willing back the sweet cloud that had enveloped them. But it was no use. The phone kept jarring the air.

Tory reached over and lifted the receiver. It was Andy. 'Is this the bag-lady illustrator?' her cheerful voice rang out.

'Oh Andy,' Tory laughed. 'You should see your friend the bag-lady illustrator. I'm now the proud owner of fifty of Vermont's prettiest acres.'

'Fifty acres? Tell this poor city-bred person, how much is fifty acres?'

'Well, I'm not too sure myself,' Tory laughed. 'Why don't you come see for yourself?'

'That's just what I was planning,' Andy replied. 'I thought I'd drive up this weekend, if I wouldn't be interrupting anything.'

Tory glanced over at Mitchell. Andy sure had interrupted something. Mitchell was sitting on the edge of the bed with his back to her. 'No,' she answered brightly, 'you won't be interrupting anything. I'd love to see you. Just bring plenty of warm clothes. My furnace isn't any too reliable.'

By the time the two friends had hung up,

Mitchell was dressed. Tory was surprised, and even a little bit hurt. She pulled the blankets up to hide her nakedness. 'My friend Andy is coming up this weekend . . . tomorrow.'

Mitchell simply nodded. 'I think I can hear the insulation calling me,' he made a lame joke. 'If I don't get that woodshed done pretty quickly, you will find me turned to ice one morning.' Then, without a backward glance, he left the room.

Tory heard the door to the woodshed slam shut, and a few minutes later the hammering began. She sat for a long time thinking about what had almost happened. Mitchell Caldwell certainly was a moody man. It was probably just as well that nothing had happened. She ran her hands up her own naked body. Bodies were dangerous things. If she could just live and operate with her mind alone, it would be much safer in the long run. Bodies lusted after bodies. Minds had much better sense. Wanting Adam's body had got her into all sorts of trouble. She didn't need to get into all that grief and hurt again. It was just as well that Mitchell was nobody, and that he had had second thoughts about making love to her. It was much better to know now that Mitchell Caldwell wasn't to be trusted. She should have known that in the first place.

Tory got up and got dressed. She didn't see Mitchell again for the rest of the day. He was there all right, the hammering went on and on.

The furnace behaved beautifully, so there was no reason to visit the woodshed. If only she could forget the feel of him beside her, the feel of his hands on her body. Well, I will forget; I must, she told herself repeatedly.

Five

Saturday morning there was a note on the kitchen table from Mitchell. 'I think we need to talk,' it said. 'See you Monday, Mitchell.'

It was definitely the note of a moody man. He was probably self-centred, and when you got right down to the nitty-gritty of it, mean too. Tory wadded up the note and threw it in the bin. Well, she didn't have to worry about Mitchell Caldwell. Andy was coming. That would be fun. She'd show her old friend how well she was adapting to life in the country. Maybe she'd even try to bake some bread. She imagined Andy walking into her snug little house with the aroma of fresh bread to greet her.

Tory dug out three cookbooks, and finally chose a recipe for potato bread. It didn't sound too difficult. Why was it people thought that baking bread from scratch was such a big deal? All you needed was flour, butter, water, yeast and in this case some mashed potatoes.

Tory had the dough mixed and kneaded before

she remembered she didn't own any bread-pans. She looked in Mitchell's cupboard. His small store of kitchen utensils was neatly stacked, including four aluminium bread-pans. She only paused a moment, and then decided he wouldn't mind if she borrowed two of them. She plunked the dough into the pans and greased the tops as the recipe instructed. Then she covered them with a dish-towel to rise.

She made the bed in the guest bedroom, dusted off Aunt Marian's oak dresser and hung the tintypes of Great Aunt Mabel and Uncle Harry. She didn't have any curtains for the windows. She hoped that Andy wouldn't be nervous sleeping and dressing in a room without something up at the windows. There wasn't another house in sight, only lovely rolling acres of snow and trees. If Andy was uncomfortable, they could rig up a sheet or something. Tory didn't want to buy curtains until she had chosen new wallpaper for the room. And at the moment with all this wiring business, she couldn't afford any of that.

By the time she had the room ready, it was time to pop the bread in the oven. She whisked the towel off the bread-pans and was very dismayed to find the dough was just the same size it had been when she first put it in. Maybe it takes longer to rise in the winter, she told herself reasonably. I'll wait another hour.

Andy surprised her and arrived just at noon. 'I got an early start,' she chirped. 'I couldn't wait to see your new digs. This is beautiful!'

Tory smiled and helped Andy carry her bags into the house. Andy always travelled heavy. She had more clothes for a short weekend than Tory had in her entire wardrobe.

Tory eyed the complete set of matching Gucci luggage. 'Oh, you know me,' Andy giggled. 'I can't bear to be unprepared. Besides that, you did tell me to bring plenty of warm clothes. I brought every warm shred I could find. I didn't know the colours of your wallpaper and paint. Since I didn't want to clash with your house, I brought enough to choose from.' Andy laughed at herself, and Tory joined in. Though knowing Andy's love of clothes, Tory wasn't altogether sure that Andy didn't mean exactly what she said.

Tory gave her friend a tour. Andy was exuberant in her praise of the old woodwork and the mellow pine floors. 'Your dream come true,' she spread her arms and her gold bracelets chimed. She gave Tory a hug. 'You're so wise, and patient. I could never have saved as you did. I'm just going to have to marry a wealthy man. What's in there?' She was pointing at the woodshed door.

'That's the woodshed,' Tory answered. For some reason she didn't really want to show Andy the woodshed and have to explain Mitchell Caldwell.

'Well, are you going to show it to me, or not? Or are woodsheds reserved for visiting royalty only?'

Tory opened the door.

'My gosh, what are you doing out here?' Andy walked into the woodshed and inspected the rolls of insulation. 'What's this stuff? It looks like stuffing for an awfully large teddy bear.' She giggled.

'That's insulation,' Tory explained.

Andy spotted the sleeping-bag in the corner. 'You sleep out here?'

'No, my tenant sleeps out here,' Tory replied, hoping against hope that Andy wouldn't ask any further questions.

'Tenant? You've got a tenant? Male or female?' Andy asked, going straight to the heart of the matter immediately.

'Male,' Tory replied, hardly above a whisper. Why was she finding this so difficult?

'Young or old?' Andy continued.

'A little older than we are,' Tory answered.

'Handsome?'

Tory nodded.

'Unattached?'

'I think so.'

'Interesting?'

Tory sighed. Andy was in the wrong business. She would have made a great lawyer. 'I guess you could say that he's interesting. Mitchell's a writer.'

'A writer! Now, that is interesting. Nice name, Mitchell. Is he a RICH handsome writer?'

'Andy!' Tory said in a warning voice.

'Now, now,' Andy chirped in her light-hearted way. 'You know me. I just want to get all the particulars straight before I meet the man.'

'Let's have some lunch.' Tory changed the subject and led the way out of the woodshed.

The bread still hadn't risen, and Tory slid the pans into the refrigerator out of the way.

The two friends munched on tuna salad sandwiches.

'Well, is he?' Andy smiled. She wasn't going to let the subject drop until Tory had answered her questions. Tory knew that, when she opened the woodshed door. She sighed. She might as well get it over with.

'Mitchell Caldwell is approximately thirty. He's handsome and I doubt very much that he has much more than two nickels to rub together. He's a writer; of what, I don't know. He's fixing up the woodshed for a room to live and write in. He's paying me rent with which I plan to buy a furnace. He's gone away for the weekend; where, I have no idea. He's only planning on staying here until his book is finished. You probably won't get to meet him. And that's absolutely all I know,' she finished in a rush of words.

Andy was regarding her friend with a calculating eye. Whatever she might have thought about Tory's touchiness on the subject of Mitchell Caldwell, she didn't say. 'Well, you surprise me, you know that? I never would have guessed that my good friend the bag lady would move to Vermont and turn immediately into a landlady.'

Tory winced inwardly at the word. That's what Caldwell had called her. She arranged her face and put on a smile. 'Yes,' she nodded her head, 'I am an enterprising young woman, busily building an empire.'

Andy took another bite of sandwich. 'You can kid all you want. But you're a whole lot smarter than I am. You'll have your empire up here in Vermont, and I, because I can't save anything, will be the bag lady living on the streets. Modelling pays well, but there's always a new young fresh face gaining on you. First thing a model knows, she gets a wrinkle or two, and she's out of business.'

Tory looked at the beautiful vibrant face of her friend and couldn't for the life of her imagine Andy as old.

'That's why I think I should marry H. Richard Merryman,' Andy continued matter-of-factly.

Tory couldn't believe her ears. 'Marry old Merryman? You're kidding, of course.' The two friends had often joked about the rich older man who had chased Andy for years.

'No, I'm not kidding. I mean it. I've made up my mind. He's kind. He's sweet to me. He doesn't expect me to do much more than decorate his life. And he can keep me in the manner to which I have grown accustomed . . . too accustomed.'

'But . . . but . . . but . . .' Tory stammered, not knowing what to object to first. 'You can't!'

'Oh yes, I can. And I will. You might as well save your breath, oh friend of mine. That's the way it's going to be.'

Tory could see that Andy was deadly serious. Gone was her usual flighty demeanour. Two sad serious eyes were meeting hers across the table.

'But what about love, doesn't that count?' Tory asked stubbornly. She wasn't at all willing to let the subject drop.

'He loves me,' Andy replied. 'And right now I think that's all that counts. Maybe that's all that ever counts. Tell me, how many happy couples do you know? Most of my friends are either divorced or thinking about it. A few are smart like you; they're happily single.'

'Happily single! You think I'm happily single?'

'Well, aren't you? You've got a good business. You're successful at it. You've just made your dream come true. You've got your home in Vermont. You don't need a man to make your life complete or to change one thing about it. So maybe it would be nice to have a nice hunk of male body to keep you warm, but you don't go around with a long face mourning the absence. You could date someone if you felt the need. And you hardly ever do. Yes, I think you're happily single!' she answered stubbornly.

'But what I seem to be, doesn't have anything to do with what you should do,' Tory answered helplessly. She could see the tight set of her friend's jaw, and knew she'd have to have a better answer than that to change Andy's mind.

'I suppose you're going to tell me that I should wait for Mr Right to come along. That I should wait to fall helplessly in love as you did with Adam.'

It was a low blow. Tory felt it in the pit of her stomach. But she also knew that if they were going to discuss this matter, then they had to pull out all the stops. 'Adam was a mistake,' she said slowly.

'Because falling in love is a mistake. Can't you see that, Tory?' Andy's voice was pleading. She wanted Tory to approve, at least intellectually, of what she was doing.

'Not always. It can't always be a mistake. What about the great lovers in history?'

'Like Romeo and Juliet?' Andy asked ruefully. 'They were children, barely teenagers. And they died. They didn't live long enough to find out if their love would have lasted. They probably would have divorced before they reached twenty!'

'You're a pessimist. My God, Andy, the world is a better place than that. Regular ordinary people marry and make love work. It happens all the time.' She grabbed the little valley newspaper. 'Here, look at this. Here's a couple that's been married for fifty years. They're all around. Knock on any door. Happy couples who fall in love and stay in love all their lives. I see their pictures in the paper every week.'

'Those are ordinary people, as you said.' Andy was speaking through gritted teeth. 'I'm not like them. I'm a top model. I make their yearly salary in one week. I buy Gucci luggage and designer clothes. I like that. I want that. I don't want to give it up.' Her voice ran down. 'Maybe I can learn to love him,' she said sadly, tears brimming her eyes.

Tory got up and went around the table to give her friend a warm hug. 'I'm sorry, Andy. I don't want to make you unhappy. If this is what you want, then be happy doing it. I just hate to see you make a mistake, that's all. Maybe you're right. Maybe too many of us believe in love in bloom and all that. And maybe it is all a pipe-dream.'

'I didn't come up here to argue with my best friend in all the world,' Andy said, drying her eyes and trying her best to smile. 'I want you to show me your fifty acres. I'm such a city mouse, that I have no idea how much land that is.'

'I must admit that I had no idea either, until the real estate people began to teach me a little. There's so much to know about living in the country,' Tory continued, trying her best to be more light-hearted than she felt.

The two friends tugged on boots and warm jackets and tramped down to the road. Tory pointed out where her land began. They walked a little way in along a hedgerow, then gave it up because the snow had drifted too deeply.

They walked several miles along the ploughed road, talking on safe subjects.

After their long walk in the cold air, they were looking forward to being back inside the warm house. Of course the furnace had gone out. Tory pushed the button and kept her fingers crossed. The furnace roared back on. With Mitchell gone, she fervently hoped the beast would be on its best behaviour. She built a fire in the woodstove just to be on the safe side.

They had a pleasant dinner, and Tory had taken another peek at her bread. Still flat as a pancake. Maybe that's what she had made — pancakes. Why was it that Mitchell Caldwell could make bread and she couldn't? The recipe was so simple. What had she done wrong? She had a sneaking suspicion that Caldwell had told his bread pans not to cooperate with her. I wouldn't put it past him, she growled to herself.

The long walk in the crisp air and the food made them both sleepy. It was just nine o'clock when they said goodnight.

As sleepy as she was, Tory couldn't get to sleep for a long time. She kept thinking about all that Andy had said. What a shame. What a waste. But then, what if she was right? Maybe love was an illusion. Maybe the only way to approach life was with one's head. She had told herself that very same thing just yesterday. Right here in this bed, after she and Mitchell Caldwell had almost succumbed to the pleasures of the body. She put out her hand and felt the coldness of the sheet beside her. What had she expected? That it would still be holding the warmth of his handsome body? Even if he had just got out of her bed, might it not still be cold? If love was an illusion, and bodies were all lust; then no matter how warm the sheet felt, it was really cold. An illusion. Life was all mirrors and magician's tricks. Things never were what they seemed at all. Today's marriage was tomorrow's divorce statistic. Maybe she had better work on being happily single.

The antique shelf-clock that had belonged to her grandfather dinged out one on the thin night air before she fell into a troubled sleep.

Sunday morning dawned clear with a blue silk sky. Tory decided that she would try her hand at making pancakes — from scratch. 'You're going to be my guinea-pig,' she told Andy. 'I don't think I can become a real dyed-in-the-wool Vermonter until I know how to make pancakes served with maple syrup.'

'You're probably right,' Andy agreed. 'I'll do my best for science.' Andy was one of those lucky people who could eat anything and still not gain an ounce. She loved to eat, but was a terrible cook. She solved that problem by going to all the best restaurants. There was hardly an elegant restaurant in New York City where they didn't greet her by name.

That's part of the problem too, Tory reflected, as she measured out flour and baking powder. Andy had really boxed herself in with the lifestyle she'd chosen. If she had been a gourmet cook, maybe she wouldn't be so tempted to marry H. Richard Merryman. If . . . if . . . if, Tory thought to herself as she greased the frying pan.

The first pancake stuck to the pan, but the next ones came out golden brown and perfect.

Tory heated some real Vermont maple syrup, and the two friends dug in.

'Scrumptious,' Andy beamed. 'If I didn't know better, I'd say you were a true born-and-bred Vermonter.'

'Thank you,' Tory smiled in return. 'What do you call him?'

'Richard,' Andy answered, just as if they had both been talking about H. Richard Merryman all along. She gave her friend a look that clearly said — be careful, please, I really don't want to discuss this.

'Oh,' Tory answered, and then changed the subject.

Tory and Andy had always referred to the round short Merryman as Friar Tuck. Friar Tuck from Robin Hood. He looked the part.

After breakfast Tory helped Andy pack her Gucci bags back in the car. The weather was due to change later in the day, and Andy wanted to get an early start back to the city. Back to H. Richard Merryman, Tory thought with distaste.

The sun was warm, almost too warm for mid-November. Everything was dripping with melting snow. The two friends stood quietly for a moment, savouring the air and the view. 'I know you'll find it hard to tear yourself away from all this,' Andy swept her arms wide. 'But do come down and visit me in the poor old city soon.'

'I will.' Tory hugged her friend.

'We're planning a small wedding,' Andy went

on. Just a few friends.' Tory was very aware of how they were both thinking along the same lines. All the thoughts they dared not speak aloud. How profoundly sad.

'You will come, won't you?' Andy's voice was almost pleading.

'Of course,' Tory answered. As much as she disapproved of what Andy was planning, she couldn't let her friend down.

Andy waved a cheery goodbye, and then took off down the hill, the car splattering the puddles all the way down the road.

Tory stood for a long while looking at the curve in the road where Andy's car had disappeared from sight.

Six

It was almost midnight. Tory was still up, sitting in the kitchen sipping a cup of cocoa. Lights came up the hill. Caldwell came in at the door. He raised his eyebrows. 'Waiting up for me?' There was a thin smile on his face, but his eyes weren't smiling.

'Of course,' Tory replied in an icy voice. Men, she was thinking, are all the same. They think we women can't live without them.

'Miss me?' he continued in the same vein.

'Don't flatter yourself, Caldwell,' Tory came back. There was a deliberate bite to her words.

Mitchell went to the refrigerator and helped himself to some cheese from his shelf. 'What's this?' He pulled one of the bread pans off his shelf where Tory had put them and forgotten them last evening. 'Looks to me as though someone was trying to make bread.'

Tory grabbed the pan out of his hand, and took the other one out of the refrigerator. 'It was just an experiment that didn't work. I'll wash up your pans . . .'

'My pans?'

Too late Tory realised that he hadn't recognised his property. Her and her big mouth. 'I borrowed your pans,' she answered lamely. 'I didn't think you'd mind. I intend to buy some of my own,' she added in a frosty voice.

'You can borrow my pans any time you want. Would you like to borrow my recipe too?' he asked, trying to look as innocent as she could.

He was so maddening. So superior. So he could make bread and she couldn't. He didn't have to rub it in. So he was handy in the kitchen, so what.

He watched her dump the still unrisen dough in the garbage. 'Tsk, tsk. Too bad you didn't have any home-made bread to offer . . . what's his name?'

Tory frowned at him. 'Who? You mean Andy?'

'Yes, I guess that was the name. Andy.'

'You think . . . oh, that's funny. For your information Andy is a female. Her name is Antonia, Andy for short.' She relished telling him. Could it be that he was jealous?

'Well, what do you know about that,' was all he said. But he seemed to relax.

The more she thought about it, the madder she got. The nerve of him. If he was jealous then that meant that he somehow figured that she, Tory, was his property. How dare he think that! If she had thought more quickly, she would have taken advantage of his mistake. She would have enjoyed seeing him squirm thinking that she had spent a glorious weekend with a man named Andy. His property, indeed!

'Here, have some cheese, landlady.' His amber eyes were now smiling.

'No, thank you, Mr Caldwell. It's late, and I have lots of catching up to do on my work. Good night.'

'Good night landlady. Sweet dreams.' He watched her go with proprietory eyes.

Tory fell immediately to sleep and dreamed of furnaces, and plumbers with leering grins, who looked a lot like Mitchell Caldwell.

She awoke the next morning none too rested. The sheets were all pulled out. She smoothed them back in place with several angry pulls and tugs. Damn that man. It was bad enough that he disturbed her waking hours; did he have to disturb her dreams as well?

She pulled on her jeans and a soft velour top in a rich Irish green. Her blond hair looked like spun gold against it. And her blue eyes took on a hint of the green and looked like two aquamarines.

She tiptoed around the kitchen, hoping to have some breakfast before the 'lovable' Mr Caldwell appeared. The coffee was only half-perked when he came whistling in. Tory was one of those people who take time to awaken in the morning. She didn't even like to talk to anyone until she'd had her coffee. Mitchell Caldwell's exuberant whistling was more than she could take.

'Please don't do that,' she said between clenched teeth.

'Do what?'

'Whistle. I like it quiet in the morning.'

'Oops, sorry. I didn't realise you were a slow starter.'

She swung around with daggers in her eyes. He put up his hands, and stepped backwards. 'Sorry. Sorry.' He couldn't hide his grin. 'Mum's the word. I promise.' And he pretended to zip his mouth closed.

He was as good as his word. He didn't utter another sound. But he watched her every move with a wide grin.

'Stop it!' Tory almost shouted.

'Stop what? I'm not whistling. I haven't even squeaked,' he added in an injured tone. The grin was still there.

'You know perfectly well what I mean. You're staring at me!'

'Watching. I was just watching. There's a difference between staring and watching . . .'

'Spare me the details,' Tory sighed. She had never known a more exasperating man in her life.

'Tell you what. I'll fix us both some breakfast. That way you can watch me. Fair enough? Would that make you happy?'

Tory let out a long sigh. She nodded her head and sat down. What would make her happy right now would have been if she had never met Mitchell Caldwell. As exasperating as he was, there was still something about him that made her very nervous and jumpy . . . in a way that she didn't like to think about or deal with. He was appealing. And her body was responding to that appeal.

'One egg or two?'

She glared at him and held up one finger.

'Let me know when it's safe to talk to you.' He turned and cracked three eggs into the frying pan. 'We do need to talk.'

The breakfast was delicious. The eggs were done just right. Much better than she could do, she had to admit. And after two cups of coffee, she was beginning to feel more like herself. She also had to admit that he was right. They did need to talk. Obviously, they couldn't go on like this. They had to get some things settled. She was the landlord, and he was the tenant. She made the decisions, and if he didn't like it, that was too bad. He could leave. The thought of him leaving made a small pain in the pit of her stomach. You're just lust, she told the pain. Go away. I won't listen to you. Heads shall prevail.

She looked up, and found Mitchell's eyes regarding her intently. 'Can we talk now?' Gone was the grin. He was serious.

Tory let out another long sigh and nodded her head. Good. At least he was beginning to get the idea of who was boss around here.

Mitchell sat back in his chair and put his hands in his pockets. 'We have a few problems to iron out. I'm sure you're aware of that. There's something going on between us that has to be settled one way or another, or neither of us will be able to get any work done.'

Tory nodded in agreement.

'Speaking for myself, there's nothing I would rather do than take you straight to bed. And I'm pretty certain, you have some of those same feelings.'

Tory started to interrupt.

'Wait. Let me finish. Then you can have your say. I have just been through a nasty divorce. I'm not ready to make any sort of commitment to anyone. I may never be. I want you to know exactly where I stand. I don't think it's fair for me not to tell you how it is with me.' He sighed. 'I've never forced myself on a woman, and I don't intend to start now. Whatever you decide will be okay with me. I want to live here . . . I need to live here, at least until my book is done. And I don't want this . . . this electricity between us to jeopardise my work.'

Tory waited for him to go on. When he didn't, she knew it was her turn. A kaleidoscope of emotions whirled through her mind. What he had said made her angry, surprised, a little bit pleased, somewhat frightened and a whole lot doubtful. She looked at him with grudging admiration. He certainly knew how to hit the nail on the head. Then for some reason, she smiled across the table at him. She hadn't known that she was going to do that. It just appeared, like the sun popping out from behind black clouds on a stormy day.

Mitchell smiled a tentative smile back at her.

'Well,' she began, 'you leave me at a loss for words. You seem to have said them all . . . but then I guess that's fair, you being a writer and all. I certainly agree that we can't go on like this. I propose a truce in this sexually charged warfare. You will be tenant working on his book. I will be landlady working on her illustrations. We shall be cordial. We might even be friends. We don't need to be lovers.'

Something inside Tory winced, as if her stomach had been chewing a lemon. There certainly was some part of her that didn't agree with the last line of her proposal. Tory ignored it. 'Agreed?' she asked.

'Agreed,' he answered with a rather painful smile. He offered a hand across the table to shake on it.

Tory gingerly shook his hand, and was dismayed to find that the electricity was still there. The feel of his skin on hers sent pleasant little tingles up her arm and down her sides. She hoped he wasn't experiencing the same thing. But of course not, she told herself, this whole business was his idea. He obviously wanted to lay the matter to rest once and for all. And she completely agreed. It would be the height of foolishness not to. Then why was it she felt as though she had just agreed to sail on the maiden voyage of the *Titanic*?

By the end of the week Mitchell had the woodshed insulated and covered with some beautiful old grey barn boards he had found in one of the outbuildings. He was very handy. He had installed a wood stove for heat, unrolled his braided rugs and hung several nice prints. The effect was rustic but warm and homely. He had even rewired the kitchen, so that Tory could now toast bread to her heart's content. Tory was well pleased. She was quite certain that the addition of the woodshed room made her little house worth more than she had paid for it. Mitchell, she noted, looked worn out. 'You ought to take a couple of days off,' she suggested one evening, when they happened to meet in the kitchen. Tory had just finished doing her dishes, when Mitchell came dragging in to make himself a sandwich.

'I plan to,' he answered. 'Just as soon as I'm done.'

'I thought you were done.'

'I want to lay some plastic down on the ground in the crawl-space under the woodshed floor. That will help keep the dampness out.'

Tory shivered at the thought of crawling around in the two-foot space under the woodshed with all the spiders and who knows what. 'Is all of this really necessary? I mean, maybe you're overdoing it.' She knew all that he did made her house worth more. But she also wasn't inclined to want him crawling around in such a dismal place.

'When it gets down to twenty below this winter, I'll be glad I did it.'

'Twenty below!' Tory had never been in

temperatures that low. 'Will the beast make it, do you suppose?'

Mitchell shook his head and shrugged his shoulders. 'I'm afraid I wouldn't like to predict. But have you noticed, since I've been working on the house, it's been much better behaved.' His eyes twinkled. 'I think we may have put some fear in its beastly soul.'

'You mean it thinks we're about to throw it out?'

'Could be. Who knows the ways of beasts?' He grinned, and Tory could have jumped right into the middle of that grin. Why did he have a grin that was so . . . so . . . so damn enticing?

'You know,' Mitchell continued between bites of peanut butter and jelly, 'Thanksgiving is next Thursday.'

'It is?' Tory had forgotten. In the jumble of moving, settling in, and getting used to her new life, Thanksgiving had completely slipped her mind.

'You going home for the holidays?' he asked.

'No, this is home. I haven't any close family. Several distant cousins in Arizona.'

'What happened to your family . . . do you mind my asking?'

'No, I don't mind. My mother and father were killed in an accident, when I was five. My grandmother raised me. But she's gone now.'

'I'm sorry.' She looked at his serious face, and saw that he really was. He wasn't just mouthing empty words of comfort. Maybe I've misjudged him, Tory thought. Maybe there's more to him than I thought.

'My mom and dad have set out to see the world since Dad's retirement. If I remember their itinerary, they should be inspecting the Great Wall of China on Thanksgiving.'

Tory smiled. 'What a way to spend your retirement. Too bad you can't join them there.'

Mitchell was rummaging around in his cabinet. He came up with a granola bar. 'Actually, they did invite me. They thought it would be good for me to get away after all the dirty mess of the divorce. I really was sorely tempted to go. But then, I decided that I had to put my life back together all by myself. No help from parents, as kind as it was intended.'

Please, please, please, Tory was saying to herself, don't tell me any more. Don't take me so far into your confidence. I might like it far too much. I might want to stay. And then when your book is done, and it's time for you to leave, I won't know how to handle it. One major heartbreak in a lifetime is enough.

As though he had read her mind, Mitchell didn't say anything more about himself. He studied her face for a moment, then finished his granola bar. 'I'm going to my sister's for Thanksgiving. She and her husband and two children live over in the Connecticut River valley. Over the mountain.' He pointed east. 'It's really not far. Pretty country too. Would you like to go with me?'

'Me?' Tory was dumbfounded.

'You'd like my sister. You remind me of her . . . not in looks, in temperament. Strong, self-reliant with a feminine courage that's quiet but always and forever there.'

Tory raised her eyebrows. Quite a handful of compliments.

Mitchell laughed good-naturedly at his own unusual generosity. 'There,' he grinned that marvellous grin of his, 'did all my flattery get me somewhere?' Before she could think of a smart comeback, he added seriously: 'I meant every word of it. And I won't take it back, even if you say no.'

Of course she didn't want to say no. She felt she should say no for the ongoing safety of their living-arrangement. But he had so cleverly worded his invitation, that she let the word 'yes' escape her lips before she had a chance to gather her common sense and say a proper no.

'Good. You won't be sorry.'

Some part of her mind was already sorry. She had a perfect right to get to know her tenant better, she argued with herself. There was nothing wrong in that. Just that he happened to be a handsome, sexy male didn't mean that they couldn't be friends. They could be friends without jumping into bed or getting emotionally involved. Of course they could.

Seven

By the time Thanksgiving arrived, Tory had argued herself in and out of going at least a hundred times a day. It was nice to be included in a family celebration, she told herself. No harm in that. But there was the problem of being with Caldwell for hours and days at a time. Try as she might, she just couldn't shake the persistent itch of wanting to touch him. Well, not just to touch him. She was being brutally honest with herself. She wanted to go to bed with the man. Every shred of common sense she possessed cried out against that very dangerous want.

I can handle this, she told herself over and over again. She packed her battered old suitcase. 'It's certainly not Gucci,' she said out loud. And that made her think of Andy. Dear Andy selling her soul, or was it just her body, for the expensive things in life. The whole idea distressed her so, that she had put off going to the city for the promised visit. Andy had called several times, practically pleading with her to come. Tory had finally agreed that she'd come shortly after the first of December. She had to see a publisher anyway, so she might just as well kill two birds with one stone. Of course she didn't tell Andy that. Andy was so happy to have her come, she could hardly contain her enthusiasm. 'You can help me pick out my wedding gown. We'll have such fun,' she trilled. 'It's no fun picking out a wedding gown without my best friend to share it with.'

Tory listened and shook her head. Andy was counting on Tory to keep her negative feelings to herself, and that put the very open and truthful Tory in a tight spot. She would have to watch every word, guard every thought that might show on her face. Andy might think it was fun, but to Tory it looked like an ordeal.

She looked at herself in the mirror. 'This could be an ordeal too, you know,' she told her reflection. 'Thanksgiving with Caldwell and Company,' she said out loud.

'Did I hear someone mention my name?' Mitchell stuck his head in the door. 'Ready?'

Tory blushed at being caught talking to herself. She turned around and fussed with her suitcase so that he wouldn't see. 'Ready,' she answered with more enthusiasm than she felt.

Mitchell filled her in with names and family details on the two-hour drive over the mountain. Sally, Mitchell's sister, and her husband Alex lived in a snug little farmhouse on the outskirts of a village. They had two children, one of each flavour, as Mitchell put it. Sara was three and big brother Josh six. Alex worked for Dartmouth College just across the river in Hanover, New Hampshire. Sally was an interior designer — on sabbatical, she had said, until Sara was in school. 'My sister has very strong feelings about mothers being home with pre-school children. You don't want to get her going on that subject, unless you want a battle royal on your hands.' He glanced over at her. 'How do you feel about working mothers?'

'I guess I haven't given it much thought,' she answered. That was only half true. She hadn't given it much thought since Adam left. Before that, she had had it all planned. She thought that *they* had had it all planned. She and Adam were going to have at least two children. And she would be able to stay home with them, of course, because her work allowed her to do that. She would have done less work and more babies, it was simple. The perfect set-up. She could have her cake and eat it too. Tory felt a lump rising in her throat. Damn! She had made a promise to herself never to cry about Adam again. She certainly wasn't going to break that promise riding through the Green Mountains of Vermont with Mitchell Caldwell.

They drove on in silence for a while, Tory getting her emotions under control, and Mitchell thinking his own thoughts.

'Oh, I almost forgot Brutus!' he smiled.

'Who's Brutus?' Tory was picturing a wild Russian uncle.

'Brutus is the dog. He's very lovable. Very large, like a giant powderpuff with legs. He's an Old English sheepdog.'

'Oh, I love sheepdogs,' Tory replied. 'They're just like overgrown teddy bears!'

'Overgrown mops, is more like it. Have you ever had one shake on you after he's been swimming in the pond? Or how about burrs? Have you ever spent half a day removing burdocks from a sheepdog's coat? Teddy bears, indeed! You are just like my sister. She thinks they're cuddly and cute too. More like a four-footed abominable snowman, if you ask me.'

'Your trouble is you're just a grouch,' Tory laughed.

'Grouch or no grouch,' he replied, 'if that dog goes swimming, take my advice and run for your life. He can drown a grown man on dry land with one magnificent shake!'

'I'll try to remember,' Tory laughed. She resisted the urge to reach over and pat him on the shoulder.

'You don't have to take my word for it. You're about to see for yourself.' He grinned at her and turned in at the next mailbox. The house sat on a little rise of land, much closer to the road than her house. But it was very nearly the twin, except this one was red.

'Look familiar?' Mitchell asked.

'I'll say. This house's mother had twins! If I

painted mine red, you wouldn't know if you were here or there.'

A pretty dark-haired woman waved to them from the door. Two children, a boy with dark hair like his mother, and a girl in golden ringlets, came speeding out to greet them. 'Unca Mitch, Unca Mitch!' They swooped down on them. Mitchell leaned over and scooped them both up in his arms.

'We havin' ourselves the biggest and bestest turkey there ever was, Unca Mitch!' Little Sara stretched her arms as far as they would go.

'Now Sara,' Josh corrected her, very aware of his three-year superiority in dealing with the world. 'You're exaggerating!' He had obviously just learned the word, and was very proud to be able to use it.

'Well, I hope it's pretty big,' Mitchell spoke in Sara's defence, 'because I'm mighty hungry! My friend, Tory here, and I have just driven through wild bear country. They outnumbered us a hundred to one, but we surrounded them and drove them off. That sort of thing really gives one an appetite!'

Sara's eyes were wide as saucers. Josh was old enough to look sceptical at the wild tale.

Sally came out to meet them. 'I don't mean to seem unfriendly. I had to check the potatoes before I could leave the kitchen. However, it looks as though you've been very thoroughly welcomed anyway.' She was as pretty as Mitchell was handsome.

Mitchell leaned over, his arms still full of children, and gave his sister a kiss. Then he introduced Tory.

'Mommy, Mommy,' Sara kept pestering.

'What is it, Sara?'

'Unca Mitch is very very hungry. He and her,' she pointed at Tory, 'fought with lots and lots of WILD bears!'

'Oh, he did, did he?' Sally shook her head and smiled at Mitchell. 'Well, the next time your niece has nightmares because of your wild stories, Mitchell Caldwell, I'm going to call you up to come right on over and explain to her that you exaggerate!'

'I knew it!' crowed Josh. 'Unca Mitch exaggerates!'

'Come on in,' Sally laughed, 'and catch your breath. As soon as Alex gets back with the pies, we'll be ready to eat. I'm hopeless in the pie department,' she explained. 'There's an elderly lady just down the road, who's a whizz-bang at making pies. She even bakes them for people who know how.'

Sally showed Tory to her room, while Mitchell and the children unloaded the car.

The interior of the house was laid out a little different from Tory's. And since Sally was an interior designer, it was stunningly painted, papered and decorated.

'Such a pretty house,' Tory enthused. 'I've got a long way to go before mine looks anything like this.'

Sally beamed. 'The first time we visited Mitchell, we were flabbergasted to see how similar the two houses were. This one lives very well. We love it. I think you'll fall in love with yours, if you haven't already.'

'I fell in love the first time I laid eyes on mine. The only fly in the ointment is a cranky old furnace.'

'Oh, we know all about cranky heating systems. For the first two years we had this, we only had two wood stoves. It didn't have a central-heating system until we could afford to put one in. I'll tell you, I learned a lot about chopping wood those first two winters. Josh was a baby, and I was so worried that he'd freeze to death. Of course he thrived.'

Mitchell and the children arrived with the bags, which they put in a corner of the bedroom. Tory had a momentary pang of worry. Certainly he wasn't planning on sleeping in here too. But she didn't have time to inquire. The children were laughing and hanging on him, asking to hear more stories. 'Tell us more bear stories, Unca Mitch,' Sara begged. Then Brutus, Alex and the pies arrived all at once.

There were more introductions. And then Sally announced it was time for the feast. It was a joyous gathering, and Tory soon felt like one of the family.

Alex was tall and blond, with kind blue eyes behind glasses. He was plainly still very much in love with Sally, and she with him. I wish Andy could see this, Tory thought wistfully. Maybe she'd change her mind about marrying old Friar Tuck.

The children had insisted that Unca Mitch sit next to them, so Mitch was between them on one side of the table, while Tory sat on the other side by herself. Brutus came and lay down beside her.

'We abide by the Brutus Rule in this house,' Alex intoned seriously, though his eyes were giving him away. 'Anything that lands on the floor is automatically his.' He dropped a half-piece of biscuit in front of Brutus. The dog vacuumed it up in an instant. 'Best automatic floor-cleaner ever invented.'

'You shouldn't feed him from the table, Alex. You're going to spoil him,' Sally frowned.

'But it's Thanksgiving, dear. And besides that, having grown up with two babies, and serving gallantly through two "Rains of Food" under the highchair, I don't think we can change him now.'

Sally grinned and shook her head. 'You're probably right.'

Little Sara was looking at Tory, her face serious in three-year-old thought. 'Are you Unca Mitch's new mother?'

'W . . . what?' Tory choked.

She looked across the table at Mitchell. He was trying his best to hide his laughter behind his napkin.

'She means wife,' Sally explained.

'No,' Tory answered. 'I'm not his mother or his wife.'

'You're just Unca Mitch's girlfriend, aren't you,' Josh added to the conversation.

Tory wasn't sure how to answer that one. All eyes at the table were on her, awaiting her answer. Even Mitchell, who was still having a hard time keeping his grin from breaking into downright laughter.

'More or less,' she answered lamely. 'We're friends.'

'See,' Josh leaned forward to talk to his sister, 'she's a girl, and she's his friend. That means that she's his girlfriend.' He smiled at his sound logical reasoning.

'I think we've got a budding lawyer on our hands,' Sally smiled.

Alex was shaking his head. 'I can't say I'm looking forward to the day when he's sixteen and wants to use the car. I might just as well save myself a whole lot of trouble and aggravation and hand the keys over right now.'

'What?' Josh asked.

'Never mind,' Sally told him. 'You'll understand soon enough.'

The meal was delicious, and the company warm and welcoming. Tory couldn't remember a time or a place where she had felt more at home. Alex and Sally were bright, intelligent people, who had made a marriage that worked very well. Andy really should see this. It does happen. It is possible. It can be done.

When it was time for the children to go to bed, they came down to the living-room to say good night. Sara put both hands on Tory's shoulders and gave her a big kiss on the forehead. 'I like you,' she said in a three-year-old's direct way. 'You should be Unca Mitch's mother.'

Tory blushed. 'Thank you. I'll give it some thought,' she whispered, hoping that nobody had overheard their conversation.

After the children had gone to bed, the two couples played Monopoly until none of them could keep their eyes open.

'That's the trouble with this game,' Sally yawned. 'It goes on and on, and nobody ever wants to stop.'

'Well, I do,' Alex stretched.

'Oh you,' Sally pushed at him playfully. 'That's only because you're winning for once. Usually I have to drag you away.'

'Well, drag me away tonight while I'm winning,' he answered grinning. 'That way, it'll give me encouragement to go on, so you can keep beating the pants off me.'

'Hmm,' Sally replied, love shining in her eyes. 'I like the way you put that.'

Alex reached over and kissed her warmly. Something in Tory melted. How she envied them their relationship.

Sally and Alex said good night and left them sitting in the living-room. 'Well, I think that's our cue,' Mitchell grinned.

'Fine,' Tory agreed. 'Now, just where are we supposed to sleep?'

'In there,' Mitchell pointed to the bedroom where their bags were.

'In there?' Tory raised her eyebrows. 'Both of us?'

'I think that's the idea,' Mitchell was still grinning.

'You mean we're supposed to sleep together?' Tory squeaked.

'My sister is a thoroughly modern woman,' Mitchell replied. 'I suppose she thinks we do it all the time.'

'And you didn't tell her any different?' Tory asked accusingly.

'She didn't ask,' he answered.

'Oh, you are infuriating!' Tory blistered.

'And you exaggerate, to borrow Josh's favourite word.'

'What are you talking about?' Tory raised her voice in a loud whisper.

'I heard you tell Sara that you'd think about being my mother.' He grinned, very content with himself.

'You are impossible!' she blazed back at him, wanting very much to say it loudly, but afraid to wake the household. 'What would you have me say to her?' she demanded.

'Oh, I don't know,' he answered. 'How about the truth? You could have said — Never in a thousand years — or — Hell could freeze over first — or — .'

'Stop it! You know I couldn't say something like that to a child who quite obviously thinks you are two hundred per cent perfect.'

'A wise child.'

'Mitchell Caldwell.'

'Down girl. I just wanted to know if you maybe liked me a little, that's all. No need to get so bent out of shape.'

Tory sighed. It was true. He could get her going at the drop of a hat. 'Yes, yes, I like you. I wouldn't have come here with you, if I didn't like you.' There, that should serve the purpose. She was well aware that there was a frighteningly big part of her that wanted to continue . . . to say more on the subject of liking Mitchell Caldwell. She forced the thoughts away. 'But just because I like you it does not mean that I intend to sleep in the same bed with you. I am not in favour of one-night stands. I thought we had this settled.'

'Just checking,' he grinned easily. 'Let me have a pillow and blanket off that bed, and I'll camp out here on the couch. You can have the bedroom all to *yourself*.'

His emphasis on the word yourself made Tory silently quake. She suddenly had a glimpse of how long and empty years of herself might be. She refused to think about it. She went into the bedroom and got a blanket and pillow and brought them out to Mitchell.

'And my suitcase?' he asked. She waited in the living-room while he went in and got his suitcase. She wasn't taking any chances. With the way she was feeling right now, it could be dangerous to get near Mitchell Caldwell and a bed at the same time.

'Good night Tory Higgins, landlady.'

'Good night impossible, Mr Caldwell.'

Tory shut the door not quite tight. It was warped. Then she undressed and climbed right into bed. She was tired. In no time at all she was sound asleep.

Eight

It was some time later when Tory awoke. She had the very definite feeling that there was someone in bed with her. She didn't remember where she was. She only knew that there was somebody or something lying next to her. She lay very still, trying to decide what to do, when a furry arm draped itself across her body. She screamed and jumped out of bed so quickly that she knocked over the bedside table.

There was a pounding of feet and Mitchell threw open the door. 'What's wrong? Tory?'

Mitchell fumbled for the lightswitch on the wall. When he finally found it, he couldn't believe his eyes. Tory was standing in the middle of the room with her flimsy nightgown torn on one shoulder. One round breast was completely exposed. And there in her bed, wondering what all the excitement was about, was Brutus!

'Oh no, oh no!' Mitchell bent over double laughing. 'I t . . . t . . . thought you said . . . no one-night stands!' He had to hold his sides he was laughing so hard.

Tory pulled up the shoulder of her nightgown. At first she was angry. How dare he laugh at her! But then, the more she looked at his helpless laughter, and the more she looked at that big dumb teddy bear of a dog lying in her bed, the funnier and funnier it seemed. Pretty soon, she, too, was laughing at the slapstick comedy of the whole situation.

When their laughter had at last run down, Mitchell hauled Brutus out of the bed. He had to haul him out, because he wouldn't come when they called him. 'He knows a good thing when he sees it,' Mitchell grinned.

'I don't know about that . . .' Tory began.

'Well, I do,' he interrupted. 'You'd better do something about covering up all your good things, or you're liable to have two anxious males in your bed.'

Tory blushed and tugged on the torn material.

Mitchell with one hand on Brutus's collar leaned over to give her a kiss on the cheek.

Tory on impulse turned her mouth to meet his lips.

Mitchell let go of Brutus and pulled her body next to his. Tory shivered as she felt the taut muscles under his pyjamas. This was asking for trouble, she told herself. Mitchell was gently running his hands up and down the smooth material of her nightgown, sending spasms of pleasure all through her body. He carefully slipped the nightgown off her shoulders and it cascaded to the floor in a silken puddle. 'Tory, you're so beautiful.' He easily lifted her and put her onto the bed. Then, he shut the dog on the other side of the door and took off his pyjamas. He didn't turn off the light, for which Tory was thankful. She loved looking at his strong body with the curling black hair on his chest. The look of him standing there, knowing that that virile male body would soon be touching hers, made her tingle all over.

He stood for several seconds just savouring the pink and white smoothness of her skin. Tory could see the heat burning in his eyes. Hers, she knew, were the blue of the flame where the fire is hottest.

Mitchell climbed in beside her. He rested his head on one elbow, and with the other hand traced paths of growing sensuality up her arms, until her nipples stood erect and tingling in their wanting. Finally, when she felt she could stand it no longer, he fell on her breasts with his lips and then gently with his teeth. The dampened heat in Tory rose higher and higher.

She ran her hands feverishly over his tight manly body. When she got to his belly, he took her hand and guided it. 'Please touch me. I need you to touch me, Tory.'

The feel of him, and the hardness of his manhood, that would soon pierce her very being, made her writhe in desire.

Mitchell spread her thighs and rolled over on top of her. The strength of him gently penetrated to the centre of her being. Then with ever-increasing thrusts, he took her spiralling higher and higher, nearer and nearer to the pinnacle of desire. Tory rode with him, rhythm matching rhythm, her body stretching out to reach the golden ring of passion spent. They burst through, pleasure erupting and melting through their veins. The explosion taken two by two, side by side, multiplied the joy to infinity.

Mitchell collapsed on the bed beside her. She brushed his damp hair off his forehead. He looked for all the world like a little boy safe in his mother's arms. And Tory wondered what his children would look like. Surely something like Josh and Sara. 'Happy?' he looked up at her.

She nodded.

'Good.' He was about to say something else, but sleep overtook him. Tory reluctantly covered his handsome body, turned off the light, and climbed back into bed.

Well, now I've done it, she told herself. She could still feel the imprint of his body on hers. And she could reach out and touch his sleeping skin. For whatever the consequences, she thought it was worth it. The great lover Adam could move over. He couldn't hold a candle to Mitchell. Mitchell made love as though it mattered that he pleased her. Adam had always taken her along for the ride.

And what about one-night stands? And what about head living and not body living? Obviously, the body has to have its day, she answered her thoughts. I can always go back and let heads rule tomorrow. What about this becoming important to you, her thoughts asked? I won't plan on it. I'll watch out. I'll be careful. Wheet! whistled the little voice in her head. Careful? You were very careful tonight! Tough, she replied. Like the commercial says — I needed that.

First thing you know, the voice went on, you'll be seeing little Joshes and Saras every time you look at him. He's not having any of that. He told you that. I know, I know. I said I'll be careful. And I will.

She drifted off to sleep touching Mitchell's skin with the back of her arm. It was marvellously comforting.

Tory slept so long and so well, that the morning sun was high in the sky before she awoke. She reached over to touch Mitchell. The bed was empty. She frowned. Had it been only a dream? No, she ran her hands down her naked body and smiled. It wasn't a dream. They had made white-hot love. She hadn't put her nightgown back on. Her nipples puckered at the memory. Her whole body seemed more alive this morning. Tory stretched her arms above her head and yawned. She wasn't going to say it out loud so that her common sense could hear, but going to bed with Mitchell Caldwell certainly had made for a good night's rest.

She was just about to get out of bed when Mitchell came in with a mug of coffee. 'Aha, sleepy head, I see you've decided to rise and shine.' He was so cheerful, and the look of him so pleased her, that she didn't have the heart to say anything about him barging into her bedroom. That could wait. She would mention it later. She couldn't have him thinking it was now all right to run in and out of her bedroom whenever he pleased. There had to be some rules about this, or, she reflected, it would get out of hand very quickly. She would not let it turn into another Adam affair. She wasn't going to let her heart get tangled around another foot loose man.

When he came in, Mitchell had left the door open, and before either noticed, Brutus had padded into the room. He came over and with great nonchalance jumped on the bed and lay down next to Tory.

'Well,' Mitchell laughed. 'A fellow can't turn his back for a minute around here, or he'll be replaced!'

'Unca Mitch,' Sara stuck her nose inside the door, 'did Brutus come in here?'

Tory pulled the sheet up to hide her nakedness.

'Yes, he did. Why don't you take him out so Tory can get up and get dressed?'

'Come Brutus!' Sara called.

Brutus just snorted, as if to say — go away kid, ya bother me.

'Come here, Brutus!' Sara called again.

'Did you find him, Sara?' Josh came running into the room.

Tory looked at Mitchell with pleading eyes.

'Come on dog,' Mitchell reached over to grab Brutus, 'I know exactly how you feel.' He winked at Tory, who was still clutching the sheet to her chest. 'You've got to vacate the premises.'

The two children came over to help tug Brutus out of the bed. Suddenly, Brutus decided to come. Sara, Josh, Mitchell, Brutus and most of the sheet went sliding off the bed on to the floor. Tory still had a grip on one part, but enough of her was showing to make it perfectly obvious that she wasn't wearing a stitch.

Mitchell hastily untangled the sheet and pulled it back up to her. He looked at her very red face. 'Come on dog and kids. We had better vamoose or the lady in the bed is liable to skin us alive and have us for breakfast.' Before he turned around to usher the children to the door, Tory saw him bite his lip.

'Mitchell Caldwell, don't you dare,' she said in no uncertain terms. He continued towards the door, his shoulders shaking in an effort not to laugh where she could see him.

The door shut behind the menagerie, and she could hear very distinctly the sound of Mitchell's laughter.

Tory sat on the bed shaking her head. She really didn't know if she should laugh or cry.

A short while later at breakfast, Sara piped up: 'Mommy, Unca Mitch's girlfriend don't wear pyjamas or a nightgown.'

'Doesn't — doesn't wear,' Sally answered, giving Tory a helpless crooked smile.

'Well,' Sara persisted, 'if she *doesn't,* then why do you always tell me I have to?'

'Tory's mother isn't here to tell her what to do,' Sally answered, hoping that would solve the problem.

'But, you're a mother,' Sara went on. 'You can tell her she's gonna catch PEE-MONIA.'

'It's gotta be HER mother,' Josh pointed his fork at Tory. 'It can't be OUR mother. Isn't that right?' He smiled at his superior knowledge.

Sally cleared her throat. 'Yes, that's right. Don't point at people with your silverware, Josh.'

'Out of the mouths of babes . . .' Alex smiled at Tory. 'I hope you'll forgive our manners.'

'Of course,' Tory answered, but her face was several shades of red.

After breakfast they all pulled on boots to take a walk. It felt almost spring-like, as they climbed the hill behind the house. The children scampered on ahead with Brutus, Josh's dark head and Sara's blond curls gleaming in the sunlight, looking so much as if they could be her children — hers and Mitchell's — that it put a pang of sorrow in Tory's heart that it could never be. Tory wondered immediately what business that thought had in her head. She shook her head to dismiss it.

They continued to walk up the hill, Alex and Mitchell walking ahead with Josh and Brutus. Little Sara came back and took Tory's hand. 'I like you,' she said and looked smiling up at Tory.

'I like you too,' Tory smiled in reply. Oh

Mitchell, what have we done, the little voice inside her head asked over and over again.

Coming back down the hill, Mitchell walked beside her. Tory wanted to touch him. Alex and Sally were holding hands and chatting in front of them. They were so natural, so right together. How lucky they were. Tory jammed her hands in her pockets to keep from reaching over to take Mitchell's hand in hers. I mustn't make this a couple thing, she told herself. I mustn't fool myself again. I am Tory Higgins and he is Mitchell Caldwell, and we had fun and games last night, but that's that. It was something that happened in a moment of time. I must not, I will not, let it climb out of that time-frame.

'A penny for your thoughts, landlady,' Mitchell looked down at her serious face. 'Enjoying yourself?'

'Yes,' she nodded.

'Good,' he answered.

'But . . . I think we should go home . . . I mean back to MY house.' She didn't want to give the impression that where they lived was their home together. It was her home. He was still her tenant. Period.

'All right.'

She was surprised that he agreed so readily. She expected him to argue with her, or at least seem reluctant.

Sally and Alex were dismayed that they had to leave so soon. 'I hope it isn't anything the children have said or done.' Sally looked worried.

'They can be so rude at times. We want them to grow up with minds of their own. But the fine line between what's good manners and bad, is sometimes hard to grasp when you're only six and three.'

Tory assured her that she hadn't been at all embarrassed by the children. She had, she said, found them delightful, which was true.

Sally and Alex warmly invited Tory to come again, any time. And little Sara seriously told Tory to take good care of Unca Mitch. 'She doesn't have to take care of Unca Mitch,' Josh shook his head at his sister's request. 'Unca Mitch is all grown up. He takes care of himself. Don't you, Unca Mitch.'

Mitchell smiled and gave both children hugs and kisses. He winked at Tory. 'Even big boys need to be taken care of sometimes,' he answered.

Sara's face lit up. It was nice to be right, when you were only three and everyone else, especially big brother, seemed to know more than you did.

Tory was silent most of the way home. So many thoughts kept swirling around inside her head. Mitchell didn't interrupt her silence. He'd look over at her now and then and smile. Whatever his thoughts, he was keeping them to himself.

Nine

It was late afternoon and already dark by the time they arrived back at the ranch, as Mitchell put it. The house was cold. The beast had done it again. Mitchell disappeared into the basement and came up half an hour later muttering unprintable words. He had finally been able to coax the beast back to life.

Tory offered to make him a sandwich, which he accepted. When she tried to do the dishes after they were finished, the water wouldn't go down the kitchen sink drain.

'Frozen,' Mitchell said in disgust.

'But it hasn't been very cold,' Tory spluttered.

'Cold enough.' Mitchell glared at the pipes under the sink. 'That blinkity-blank furnace must have turned off the minute we drove out of the yard. If I didn't know better, I'd think it had a mind of its own — a fiendish one at that.'

'What do we do now?' Tory asked, with visions of hauling water to and from the kitchen all winter dancing through her head.

'Do you have a hair-dryer?'

'Hair-dryer? What about my sink?'

Mitchell gave her a sour look. 'Do you or don't you?'

'I do.'

'Good. Get it — please.'

If he hadn't added the please, Tory wouldn't have budged. As it was, when she brought it back to the kitchen, she slammed it into his hand. 'Here!'

He grimaced.

Serves you right, Tory thought. This live-in handyman arrangement had been his idea, and now he was being a grouch about it. It wasn't her fault. She stood with her arms crossed, frowning. Mitchell was trying to prop the dryer under the sink so that its hot air would blow directly on the frozen pipes. The cans of cleanser he was using to hold it in place kept slipping.

'You could put it in my mixing-bowl and hold it in place with several dish-towels,' Tory suggested.

Mitchell nodded. 'Worth a try.'

After he got the dryer set up, using Tory's suggestion, he stood up wearily. 'Look, I'm sorry. I don't mean to be such a grouch. It's just that two years of that furnace and its shenanigans are enough to try anyone's patience.'

'I understand,' she replied coolly. She wasn't going to let him off the hook quite that easily. Besides that, it was best that they be cool to each other. Last night was heat enough to last a long

long time. In this house things would be cool. Cool and safe. It was much easier not to think of how warm and inviting it was in Mitchell's arms. It was easier not to remember the heat of his bare body on hers. It was easier to think cool and be cool.

They waited for the hair-dryer to do its stuff. Tory stared at the curling dark hair on Mitchell's arms, where he had turned up his cuffs to work. Her memory filled in the rest of the muscular arms and back, the chest with its fine dark mat of hair. She could see the hair trailing down to the flat stomach. And then below that, the hair starting again . . .

'Tory?'

'No!' she almost shouted, startled out of her daydream.

'No?' he asked perplexed.

'Oh,' she looked aside, not daring to look him in the eyes. 'I'm sorry. What were you saying? I was thinking of something else.' She smiled a thin smile, hoping it would cover the situation.

'I just wanted to thank you for coming to Sally's and Alex's with me.'

'They're a nice couple. It was fun.' She wasn't going to be tricked into saying that she wanted more of what they had last night. 'Great kids and a crazy dog.'

'It really makes me wonder, you know.' Mitchell was shaking his head.

'What's that?'

'How they do it. They seem so happy with each

other. Not seem, they are happy with each other. They've been married eight years, and they like each other, as much now or more than they ever did. I wish I knew their secret. It makes me damn envious.'

'I know what you mean.'

'Though, I don't suppose I'd be able to handle it, whatever it is one has to do, to make a marriage work.'

'Me either,' she answered, though the little voice inside her head was strongly disagreeing.

He didn't seem to hear her. 'Or at least I wasn't able to,' he added more to himself than to her.

The sink started to blub blub blurp. The water disappeared down the drain with a sigh.

'You did it!' Tory cheered.

'Of course,' Mitchell answered with a put-on superior air. 'I'm a whizz at frozen sinks and dastardly furnaces — not so hot at marriage,' he added darkly.

He handed Tory back her hair-dryer, being careful not to touch her hand. 'Night, landlady. I've got a book needs reading. And tomorrow, one that needs writing. If you don't see me for several days, don't get worried. I've only climbed into my lonely writer-trying-to-get-his-book-done hole.' He smiled and gave her a funny little salute.

Tory watched him go. He was doing exactly what she'd hoped he would do. He was being the perfect tenant. Why was it she felt so like going after him to ask — isn't there anything more you should be doing? Like touching your landlady in all the right places?

She shook her head at her own thoughts. Boy oh boy, it was an awfully good thing that he had some common sense. Because hers for the moment seemed to have blown away.

The phone rang before Tory was up the next morning. It was Andy. 'Did I wake you up?'

'No,' Tory lied, and knew her just awakened voice gave her away.

'I thought you'd be up with the cows and pigs and stuff up there,' Andy giggled. 'You know, keeping farmer's hours.'

'I'm not totally acclimatised yet,' Tory laughed. 'But I'm working on it.'

'I called to give you an early-morning report on your former home city. Rockefeller Center is glistening in all its Christmas finery. The tree is bigger and better than it's ever been. Lord and Taylor's windows are full to popping with elves and mechanical dolls that cuddle and coo. And your good friend Andy is just about going crazy wondering when her good friend is coming down here to hold her hand and help her shop for her wedding.'

Tory laughed. 'When do you want me?'

'Two weeks ago yesterday,' Andy answered without missing a beat. 'But later today would be fine.'

Tory peered through the gloom of her early-morning room at the little lighted alarm clock on her dresser. Quarter to seven. There was plenty of time to pack a suitcase, put her drawings together, and catch the New York train that left in the early afternoon. If Caldwell could be pried loose from his writer's hold, as he called it, he could give her a lift to the station.

'If all goes well at this end,' she answered, 'you can expect me by early evening.'

'You mean it!' Andy was elated. 'You mean, you're really going to come today!'

Andy continued to bubble over with excitement. She would have gone on and on listing wedding details, if Tory hadn't reminded her that she had lots to do at this end to get ready to come.

'Right!' said Andy. 'Of course. Oh, Tory, I'm so excited. I can't wait for you to get here. I've got so much to tell you!'

Tory hung up the phone as though it were a strange unknown instrument. What was going on? Had she heard correctly? Or was she just misinterpreting? It sounded as though Andy was happy to be marrying Friar Tuck . . . H. Richard Merryman, she amended. She had better start to think of him as H. Richard or Richard. It wouldn't do to let her tongue slip and call him Friar Tuck to his face. No. Andy was probably just in love with the idea of being married to a wealthy man. She couldn't be in love with that rolypoly little man, could she?

Tory waited until nine o'clock to go knocking on Mitchell's door. She didn't relish the thought of getting him out of bed and having to look at him in his pyjamas.

He opened the door. 'The beast gone off again?'

'No,' Tory answered. 'I have a favour to ask you.'

'Yes?'

She cleared her throat. 'I know you're busy, and I wouldn't bother you except I find I need a lift to the station this afternoon. I was wondering if you could give me a lift?'

'Back to New York?'

'Yes.'

'Country living getting too much for you already?'

She frowned at him. She couldn't tell if he was teasing her or not. 'It's only for a few days. A friend is getting married and wants me to help her pick out a dress.'

'Women,' he snorted. 'They always make such a big supercharged occasion out of weddings. With fifty per cent of today's marriages ending in divorce, it seems to me the money could be better spent than on satins and ribbons that nobody will ever use again.'

Tory was getting hot under the collar. 'I don't see that it's any of your business, Mr Caldwell. I merely asked a simple favour. Either you will or you will not give me a lift to the station. It doesn't require a lecture on the merits of marriage!'

He laughed. 'You're right! Yes, dear landlady, I

will be happy to escort you to the station. Writers are always looking for excuses to get away from the typewriter, didn't you know that?' He gave her a wicked wink. 'Your carriage shall be waiting at noon, m'lady.' With that, he shut the door.

Tory stood staring at the door. He certainly wasn't an easy person to figure out. No wonder he was divorced. He must have been very difficult to live with. Lucky for her that she was getting to see exactly what he was like before she got herself any further involved with him, or thought about getting involved with him.

At five minutes to twelve, Tory and her suitcases and illustration case were at the kitchen door. She nervously eyed the closed door to the woodshed. Maybe she should remind Caldwell of the time. She hated to have to rush like mad at the last minute. She was about to knock when Caldwell emerged. 'Think I'd forgotten?' he asked.

'No,' she lied.

'Good. Let's mount up and be on our way.'

The weather had turned cold and a strong wind was blowing. The sky was full of clouds. 'Looks like a storm blowing up.'

'Snow?' Tory asked.

'I wouldn't be surprised,' he answered. 'Good thing you're leaving today. We might get snowed in for a couple of days. Good weather to sit by the fire and write.'

'Speaking of writing, what do you write?' Tory asked.

He turned his head to look at her before he answered. 'Love stories.'

'You write love stories? You're kidding, of course.'

'No, I'm not kidding. I write under the name of Valerie Valentine.'

'Come on, Caldwell, come clean. What do you write?'

'I'm not kidding. I write love stories.'

'You write about love and romance and hearts and flowers and MARRIAGE? I don't believe you.'

'Suit yourself. But that is the truth. Not only do I write love stories, but I'm very good at it too. You don't have to be good at love personally to know what people want to hear. It is possible to write about all sorts of things you've never done or will do. You must know that.'

'I suppose so, but . . .'

'No buts about it. You don't suppose Charles Dickens had to become a ghost to write about the ghosts that haunted Scrooge, do you? Or how about Margaret Mitchell?'

'Margaret Mitchell?'

'She's the creator of Scarlett O'Hara — *Gone With The Wind*. Or how about Shakespeare . . .'

'Okay, okay. I get your point. Still . . .'

'You don't see me as a romance writer.'

'Right.'

'There are probably a lot of things you don't see about me, Ms Higgins.'

'Undoubtedly, Mr Caldwell.'

'Or I about you, for that matter.'

'Obviously.'

The station loomed ahead. There were a number of other cars in the parking-lot with people waiting for the New York train. Mitchell switched on the radio. He slumped down in the seat and drummed his fingers on the steering-wheel in time to the music.

Tory sat more or less in shock. Imagine. Mitchell Caldwell wrote romances! The world was surely full of strange things.

'You'd better give me your phone number,' Mitchell reached into his glove compartment for a pencil. He was very careful not to touch Tory.

Tory wasn't sure she liked the idea of giving Mitchell Caldwell her phone number. 'Why?'

'What if something goes wrong at the house? I might need to get in touch with you. Don't worry,' he gave her an exasperated look, 'I wouldn't dream of pestering you or your marriage-minded friend unless it was extremely important.'

Tory wrote down Andy's number and put the paper and pencil on the dashboard. She'd be darned if she'd hand it to him. Right now all she wanted to do was get away from the exasperating Mitchell Caldwell.

When the train came into view, the people began to emerge from their cars. Mitchell helped her carry her luggage to the train. Her hand brushed his as he handed the bag and illustration case over to her. 'Tory . . . ?' he said quietly.

She looked up into his eyes. There was something soft there, and then it left. He changed his mind. 'Yes?'

He stepped back a pace and smiled a half-smile. 'Have a good time, landlady. Don't worry about the beast.'

Ten

All the way to New York Tory thought about Mitchell Caldwell. She tried to read a book, and thoughts of him interrupted. She slammed the book shut. Even being away from the man, she couldn't be away from him. What the devil was there about him that intrigued her so? And he was a writer of romances. That was a hot one. If there was anyone in the world who shouldn't be a writer of romances, it was the jaded Mitchell Caldwell. What did he know of romance? The man who didn't want to be committed to anyone? Why, he probably had made love to her so that he could have some new twist to put in one of his books. He'd better not. If there was anything about their night together that showed up in one of his books, she'd sue the pants off him. She felt her cheeks flush. Sue the pants off him. That was certainly apropos. She could see his fine masculine body. How taken in she had been. That was probably his game. Lucky him to have such a nice body to parade around in front of women. All he had to do was wait until someone fell into his net. And then, there he had it. Ready made. A new love story. Of course. That was why he said he was so good at it!

When I get back, she told herself, I'll throw him out of my house. Furnace or no furnace. I'm not going to be romantic grist, fodder for his writing.

Tory lay back against the seat and closed her eyes. Adam had taken her in, and now Caldwell was playing games with her. And what if he isn't, the little voice inside her head asked. You can't be sure, it went on. I don't have to be sure, she answered herself. I just have to be careful and safe.

She fell into a dream-filled sleep where Adam became Mitchell and vice versa. The furnace in the basement became a real beast, a fire-breathing dragon that stuck its head out of the hatchway and leered at her whenever she looked out of the window.

'Miss, Miss. Are you all right?' The conductor was shaking her shoulder. Tory awoke with a start.

'W . . . what?'

The conductor was kindly and old. He smiled at her. 'You must have been having a nightmare. Come on, wake up. We're in New York.'

Tory looked around. The compartment was almost empty of passengers. The last few were filing out of the door. Out of the window she could see the dim lighted interior and the platforms at Grand Central Station.

'You all right?'

'Yes, yes. I'm fine. Thank you. It was only a dream. Thank you.'

He waited while she got her bag and illustration case.

'Thank you,' she said again.

'You take care, Miss.'

'I intend to do just that,' she smiled at him.

The streets of New York were bustling with people, the shop windows bright in their declarations of Christmas approaching. Tory caught a cab to Andy's apartment. She couldn't believe that it was possible, but New York seemed more frantic and crowded than she remembered. She was more than ever thankful for her peaceful patch of Vermont. If only she didn't have the problem of Caldwell. Well, she reflected, that would solve itself, once spring arrived — if not before. She just needed a little patience, that was all.

Andy was overjoyed to see her. She swept Tory into her apartment, and couldn't stop chattering about her wedding plans. Tory had to admit that she had never seen her friend so happy. Poor Andy. Sure, it was fun getting all the satins and ribbons, as Caldwell had called them, but what happened afterwards? Afterwards, when it was Friar Tuck day after day, and night after night. Surely, she wouldn't be so happy then. Being Mrs Friar Tuck might have its advantages in the money department, but what about the department of the heart? But then, she reminded herself, maybe there wasn't much to recommend the department of the heart. She certainly couldn't say much for it personally. To love was to get hurt. Maybe Andy had the right idea. Tory sighed.

'What?' Andy turned and really looked at Tory for the first time.

Tory shook her head. 'I didn't say anything,' she smiled a weak smile.

Andy frowned. 'What's wrong?'

'Nothing,' Tory replied.

'Don't tell me nothing,' Andy came back. 'I am your oldest friend, Victoria Higgins, and I can certainly tell when something's wrong. Now, what's wrong? Is there trouble in paradise up there in Vermont?'

'No, not really,' Tory hedged.

'And what does "not really" mean?'

Tory could see that Andy wasn't going to be put off with half-baked answers. 'I just found out that my boarder is a romance writer.'

'You mean the fellow who lives in your woodshed?'

Tory nodded.

'And?'

'Isn't that enough?'

'Should it be?'

'I don't know,' Tory faltered. 'I just think it's a strange way for a man to earn a living, I guess.'

'Does he pay his rent on time? Is he quiet? Does he have friends who visit at all hours of the night?' Andy ticked off a list on her carefully manicured fingers.

'He's the perfect boarder.'

'Then, I don't see what the problem is, unless of course he's madly lusting after your body and plans to include you in one of his books.'

'Something like that,' Tory replied weakly, her face getting pink at the thought of Mitchell's body. The person lusting, she knew, was more likely herself, but she didn't add that.

'Then, you simply throw him out,' Andy answered.

'I can't . . . I mean, I could . . . well, it's not as easy as that.' Tory explained about the beast in the basement and her money situation.

'Well,' Andy replied, 'your problems will be over when spring comes. You can lock your bedroom door until then.'

Tory didn't explain that it was the woodshed door that should be locked. 'I guess so,' she replied lamely.

Andy had already dismissed the problem, and had begun to tell Tory about some of the wedding dresses she had seen, when she had a second thought. 'What sort of romance stories does this guy write?'

Tory smiled. Andy had the sort of mind that bounced from one subject to another and then back again. 'I don't know. He didn't say. He only said he used the name Valerie Valentine.'

'Valerie Valentine!' shrieked Andy, her eyes alight with delight. 'Valerie Valentine is only my favourite romance writer! I've got every book she ever wrote!'

'He,' Tory corrected.

'He,' Andy repeated. 'She, I mean, he's fantastic. He's bright and funny and understands women so well! Tory, you are a lucky person to have the Great Valerie Valentine in your very own house, under your very own roof!'

'Yeah,' said Tory half-heartedly.

'No, I mean it. Have you ever read any of her — his novels?'

'No,' Tory replied.

'Come with me,' Andy commanded. She led Tory to her bookcase. There in a line were a dozen or more books with the name Valerie Valentine on their spines. 'Here's my collection,' Andy said proudly. 'You should read them. Maybe you'd feel differently about your Michael then.'

'Mitchell,' Tory corrected.

'Do you suppose he'd autograph my books for me?'

Tory had to smile at her irrepressible friend. She looked at the impressive line of books by Caldwell. He must be good, as he said, or he wouldn't have had that many books published. Maybe she should read one or two. She took one to please Andy. She could decide later whether to read it or not.

Tory settled into Andy's luxurious guest-room.

The view out of the window was of Central Park. Even in its December bareness, it was restful to see stretches of grass and trees in the midst of the teeming city.

The two friends had a late dinner at a small French restaurant just around the corner from Lincoln Center. The food was superb. Tory sipped her wine and listened to Andy outline tomorrow's activities.

By the time they got back to the apartment, it was late. Tory took a quick bath in the deep porcelain tub. She watched her naked body in the full-length mirror mounted on the back of the bathroom door. Was this body about to appear in print in one of Caldwell's books? Her already rosy complexion got rosier still. Not if she could help it. Caldwell would find himself in a heap of trouble if that's what he had in mind.

She slipped into her nightgown and enjoyed walking across the warm thick rug in her bare feet. Andy certainly did know about the better things in life.

Her eye caught sight of the Valerie Valentine book on the bedside table. Should she, or shouldn't she? No, she decided. I'm too tired. I need my sleep to keep up with Andy tomorrow. If I start reading Caldwell now, it will probably make me angry. And if I get angry, I won't be able to sleep.

As it was, she didn't sleep too well. Mitchell Caldwell kept parading nude through her dreams. She'd turn away, so she didn't have to look at his fine male body. And then she'd find herself turning around and looking anyway. It was very frustrating.

Andy came in to wake her in the morning. 'Rise and shine, Country Gal. We've got things to do!' She was so cheerful that Tory tried very hard not to let her cloudy mood show through.

Before she left the apartment, she stuck Caldwell's book in her bag. If there was any time today, she might take a peek at it.

Andy took her from store to store. In each place the saleswomen knew her by name. Tory reflected that it was quite something for New York salespeople to remember someone's name. They had so many customers, that to be remembered in the faceless crowd took some doing . . . or buying.

They looked at so many wedding gowns, that they soon began to run together in Tory's mind. 'Well, which one do you think I should get?' Andy asked.

'They're all so beautiful, I guess you should settle on the one that you feel most comfortable in,' Tory answered, hoping that Andy wouldn't try to pin her down. She couldn't for the life of her remember which was which.

'I was thinking that I should have a long dress,' Andy went on, 'but I think I like the short lace dress at Bergdorf's best. I'm such a traditionalist, that I kept thinking I ought to go with the long one. But now with your help,' she positively glowed, 'I think I'll go with the short one.'

Tory was beginning to feel a little guilty. This was so important to Andy, and she, Tory, wasn't giving it the attention it deserved. She did her best, but her attention kept wandering. The little paperback book in her bag kept drawing her mind away from the matter of picking wedding dresses. Her bag seemed to radiate heat from the pages that were waiting inside. Of course she knew that was just her imagination, but the more her mind slipped away to think about it, the more she seemed to notice the heat coming through the leather.

After lunch, they went to look at wedding invitations. The salesperson had them sit down and then brought out huge book after huge book of sample invitations. Tory looked at the stack of sample books in agony. Did Andy really expect her to look through each and every one? Suddenly, she had an inspiration. 'Andy, why don't you look first and select the ones you like best, then I can help you make a final choice.'

'Fine,' Andy answered. 'I knew you'd be a big help. You're so organised.' She frowned. 'But what are you going to do while I'm looking? It'll be such a bore for you to just sit.'

'Don't worry about me,' Tory smiled. 'I brought along one of Caldwell's books. That should keep me occupied.' She felt a little guilty, but right now her mind wasn't worth two cents anyway.

'Oh good. You'll be impressed. You wait and see. He's super!'

Tory reached into her bag with as much nonchalance as she could muster. Her hands were shaking. Oh damn, she thought to herself, and was glad to see that Andy was already busily leafing through the sample books.

Tory read three pages. He was good, there could be no doubt about it. Well, anyone can write three good pages. She read on until she came to the first intimate encounter between the hero and the heroine. Her face began to feel hot and her hands were sweaty. Before the characters in the book could complete their love-making, they were interrupted. Tory's eyes raced on, wanting to get to the next intimate part as quickly as possible. She was tempted to look ahead, to skip pages, but she didn't want to miss anything. Tory looked up. Andy was regarding her with a thoughtful expression on her beautiful face.

'Well?'

'You were right . . . so far,' Tory hedged. She wasn't about to give Caldwell heaps of credit for forty-seven pages.

'I knew you'd like it.' Andy beamed and went back to her sample books.

Tory read on. She had just reached a part that seemed to be leading up to a love scene, when Andy turned around again. 'I've got four picked out. See what you think.' She looked at her friend's avidly interested face. 'That is, if you can tear yourself away.' She giggled.

'Of course I can tear myself away,' Tory

answered. She closed the book and put it carefully back in her bag. She forced her mind to concentrate on wedding invitations. It was hard to do, she kept having to mentally run after her attention. It kept wandering back to the story in Caldwell's book.

Tory wasn't able to get back to the book until they returned to the apartment in the late afternoon. They were going to have dinner with H. Richard. Tory wasn't exactly looking forward to that. Andy went to her room to rest a little and get ready. That left Tory with time to read before she had to get dressed.

Tory shut the door to her room and sprawled across the bed with Caldwell's book. She was soon lost in the grip of the story. The hero, who couldn't possibly be Caldwell — he was too obviously in love with the heroine — was undressing the heroine. Tory's thighs ached with the fever the words set up in her. In her imagination she was the heroine and the hero was . . . who? Not Adam. And certainly not Caldwell. But the description of the love scene made Tory remember all too well the feel of Caldwell on her skin, the electricity of his touch came back so strongly, that Tory almost felt him there beside her.

When the hero and heroine at last reached the climax of their passion, Tory rolled over and shut her eyes. There were tears on her cheeks. 'Damn you, Caldwell. Damn you.'

She was able to finish the book with five minutes to spare to dress for dinner. She threw on her clothes, with the story of the book racing through her mind and heart. How could Caldwell do it? The book had a happy ending. The hero and heroine were to be married. They believed in love. They believed in marriage. There was no foreshadowing of doom in the two hundred pages. It was a lovely story of love in bloom, of true love found. And Mitchell Caldwell, who didn't believe in such things, had written it. It wasn't fair. He shouldn't write such things. He should write what he believed. His book should have an unhappy ending . . . and so they lived unhappily ever after. 'You're a fraud, Mitchell Caldwell.' She glowered at her own image in the mirror.

Eleven

Tory heard the doorbell chime. That would be H. Richard Merryman. She tried without too much success to put on a welcoming face. She owed it to Andy to at least try to like the man.

The dinner went fairly well. Andy was her bubbly best. Richard was funny and pleasant. He very obviously wanted Tory to approve of his coming marriage to Andy. Actually, he was a whole lot better than Tory had dared hope. He was certainly in love with Andy, and if Tory hadn't known better, she would have sworn that Andy was in love with him. Any outsider watching the engaged couple would have smiled. They were nice together. But that didn't take away Tory's reservations about the whole situation.

Later, back at the apartment, Tory's eyes kept straying to Andy's Valerie Valentine collection. She sipped an after-dinner brandy with Richard and Andy and tried to keep up her end of the conversation. But her mind kept asking about the books. Mitchell's books . . . Should she allow herself to read another? The first one certainly hadn't made her any too happy. But what had Caldwell written in those other books? Had they all happy endings? Probably. Who in their right mind would want to read a romance that had a sad ending? And didn't she owe it to herself to know all she could know about a man who lived in her house? She should at least read one more. That decision made, she could hardly wait for Richard to leave, and Andy to say good night.

Richard left and Tory repressed a sigh of relief.

'Well, what do you think . . . really think of him?' Andy asked. She asked it in a light-hearted voice, but Tory knew she was totally serious.

'He's nice,' Tory said. She wanted to make Andy happy, but she wanted to reserve some judgement until she had seen more. She wondered just what she would have said had she completely disapproved. Would she have had the courage to tell Andy?

'Just nice?' Andy asked and fluffed a pillow.

'No, not just nice,' Tory responded. 'He's obviously very much in love with you. That's more than nice.'

'Yes, it is, isn't it?' Andy beamed. 'I'm so glad you approve. It means a lot to me to have your blessing.'

Whoa, wait a minute, Tory wanted to say. I didn't say I approved. But she didn't say it. She couldn't say it to Andy's beaming face.

Andy went to bed, humming a bright and happy little tune. She wished Tory sweet dreams.

Tory chose another of Caldwell's books, then she stayed up half the night reading. This story took place in Paris. The hero and the heroine played out the story of their love against the backdrop of Paris, lovely romantic Paris.

Tory wondered if Mitchell had been to Paris. And had he, like the hero, found someone to love there? The love scenes made Tory's whole body ache with desire. Every touch she could feel. With every kiss she remembered the softness of Mitchell's lips on her skin. When the hero caressed the heroine, she could feel Mitchell's strong fingers tracing lines of pleasure on her tingling body. She knew one thing for certain, Mitchell Caldwell knew how to make love to a woman . . . in the pages of a book . . . and in person.

It was the wee hours of the morning before Tory finished the second book. She fell into a dreamless sleep.

Andy again was up before Tory and knocking on her door. 'Wake up, wake up!' she sang out. 'I've brought you coffee and a doughnut.'

'Come in,' Tory managed to say, her voice still groggy with sleep.

Andy came in and perched on the edge of the bed. 'What's this?' She held up Caldwell's book. 'You read this one too?'

Tory nodded, and silently reproached herself for leaving it on the bed.

'He's fantastic, isn't he? Best writer on the market. Of course that's just my humble opinion. What do you think?'

'He writes very realistically,' Tory said slowly, carefully choosing her words. She hoped Andy wouldn't ask too many questions.

'Don't forget to ask him if he'll autograph at least one book for me.' She smiled radiantly. 'I still can't believe that he lives under the same roof with you. You're so lucky!' Happily, she didn't ask Tory if she thought she was lucky to have Mitchell Caldwell in her house. She launched into a list of things that they had to do today. There were caterers to see, and food to choose. Tory had to have a very special dress as maid of honour. And then, there was the matter of finding a suitable chapel for the marriage. Tory felt inundated. It had never really occurred to her how many things there were to plan and pick and choose for a wedding, even a small one.

Tory drank the coffee and ate the doughnut, and hoped she'd have strength enough to make it through the gruelling tasks that Andy was setting for her. 'I'd like to have some time to see my publisher too,' she added between bites.

'Of course, of course,' Andy replied.

The phone rang and Andy got up to answer it. Shortly, she came back. 'It's for you. It's Valerie Valentine,' she grinned. 'I asked him if he'd be good enough to autograph a book for me. He's so nice! So gracious! He said he'd be happy to do any favour at all for a friend of Tory's.'

Tory raised her eyebrows and went to answer the phone. 'Hello?'

'Tory, this is Mitchell. Remember me? Your

housemate up in the wilds of Vermont?'

'Yes, yes,' Tory answered impatiently. She was in no mood for games with Mitchell Caldwell. 'What's the problem?'

'How do you know there's a problem?' he asked innocently.

'Because you said you'd call me only if there was a problem,' she answered tersely.

'Maybe I'm just lonely,' he replied. 'Maybe I miss you.'

'Come on, Caldwell, out with it. What's the problem?'

'Okay, Higgins,' he answered in kind. 'You're right, there is a problem. The furnace seems to have blown up.'

'Blown up! My God, is the house still there?'

'All you can ask about is the house? Aren't you worried about whether I'm still here?'

'Obviously, you're still there, I'm talking to you,' she answered.

'But I could be burned beyond recognition. I could be swathed in bandages from one end of my body to the other . . .'

'Caldwell,' she interrupted, 'tell me about my house!'

'Your house is fine,' he answered. 'I just wanted to ask you if I should go ahead and purchase a new beast.'

'A *new beast!*'

'Unless you want to heat the house with the wood stove all winter, I think you'll need a new furnace.'

'Oh great! Caldwell, I can't afford a new one. I don't have the money!'

'I think I can afford to pay for it. I just got an advance. You could pay me back . . . or let me stay long enough to let my rent equal the price. What do you want to do?'

Tory could have torn the phone out of the wall. She wanted to strangle Mitchell Caldwell. Her common sense told her that the furnace blowing up wasn't his fault, but all the same she was very angry at him. Angry at his humour. Angry at being forced to put up with him in her home. And angry at him for the novels he wrote, that made love seem so easy and right. But instead of saying any of those things, she simply replied: 'Do what you think is best.'

'Okay, landlady, will do.' There was a pause. 'You got all the satins and lace out of your blood yet?'

'None of your business, Caldwell!'

'Right. See you when you get here.'

'Goodbye Caldwell.'

'Goodbye Higgins.'

Andy had been listening to Tory's end of the phone conversation. When Tory hung up, Andy regarded her with questioning eyes. 'The beast blew up!' Tory explained.

'The beast blew up?' Andy asked.

'My furnace,' Tory explained further.

'Oh,' Andy looked down at the floor. 'Weren't you a little hard on him?' she asked gently.

'It's necessary. Take my word for it. He's an

arrogant son of a gun.' The words were no more than out of her mouth than Tory began to regret them. Mitchell Caldwell wasn't arrogant. If he were, she reflected, it would be easier to handle him — to dislike him.

'That's too bad,' Andy frowned. 'Somehow it doesn't seem possible that the person who writes those beautiful love stories could be arrogant.' She raised her eyebrows in question.

'Well, maybe arrogant is the wrong adjective,' Tory allowed. 'Let's just say he's difficult.'

'What man isn't?' Andy smiled. 'That makes me feel much better.'

Before they left for the day's shopping expedition, Tory slipped another of Caldwell's books into her bag.

'Aren't you afraid you'll overdose on your "difficult" lodger?' Andy grinned.

'Not at all,' Tory replied frostily, not in the least amused. 'I just think it's wise to know all I can about someone who's living in my house, that's all.'

'That's probably true,' Andy answered. If she thought anything else, she didn't let on. It was very easy to see that the subject of Mitchell Caldwell was a sore spot with her friend.

It wasn't until they got to the caterers in the late afternoon that Tory had a chance to look at Caldwell's book. Andy was discussing food with the caterer, and Tory sat in a lounge chair to wait.

The setting for this romance was the island of Jamaica. All these marvellous places! She wondered if Caldwell had been to Jamaica too. He certainly wrote about it convincingly. Not that she had been there, and so had a basis for comparison. It just rang so true, that she had a hard time thinking that he might have sat in a dry and dusty library somewhere researching all he needed to know about the island of Jamaica. Montego Bay, Half Moon Bay, the Blue Mountains and the Cockpit Country. It all sounded so exotic and romantic.

The heroine in the story was blond and blue eyed. Her name was Terry. Tory had no problem imagining herself as the heroine. She was soon lost in the story, rafting down a rain-forest river with the handsome hero.

When she got to the first sensual love scene, her temperature began to rise. The heroine was tickling the hairs on the hero's chest. Her hand moved lower and lower. Tory could see in her mind's eye the fine flat belly of Mitchell Caldwell. The hero took her hand and guided it to the centre of his pleasure. 'Please touch me. I need you to touch me, Terry,' he said. Tory's blood pressure rose several points. That's what Caldwell had said to her. How dare he!

She read on with fire in her eyes. The hero gently parted the heroine's thighs and penetrated her with a thrust of his manhood. Together they moved, like a symphony of melodies, blending bodies in perfect tune with each other. The world had melted away, and they were spiralling on and on, closer and closer to the heights of passion.

Tory's thighs ached. She squirmed in her seat. At last they breached the pinnacle of desire. Tory could feel the warmth spread through their bodies like sun-warmed honey . . . just as Caldwell had written it. They lay drained side by side on the sand, while the crystal-clear waters of the Caribbean lapped at their feet.

Tory closed the book. Ah marvellous, she thought. Then her pleasure just as swiftly turned to anger. She had a Don Juan under her roof! He had to have been there in Jamaica with that woman! Just as he had been in Paris in the second book, and in New York in the first. What a fool she had been to go to bed with the man! She would probably be reading about herself in the next Valerie Valentine book that came out. Caldwell was probably right at this minute typing away, grinning to himself. He had the perfect set-up! She had been so blind. The research for his next book was living in the same house with him! Tory threw the book across the room. It skidded across the floor and thumped into the wall.

Andy turned around and looked for the cause of the sound. Then she looked at Tory. 'What's wrong?'

'Nothing. Everything!' Tory grumbled, and went over to retrieve the book. 'Caldwell's a farce, a cheat, and a liar!'

'I see,' was all that Andy replied. She wisely decided to discuss the matter later when they were alone.

The caterer, who had been watching the whole performance, looked slightly scandalised. He cleared his throat, and with great diplomatic aplomb, decided it was best to ignore unpleasant outbursts from strange young ladies.

Later in the taxi Andy brought up the subject of Caldwell. 'I don't know what's bothering you, Tory. Why is Caldwell such a sore spot with you?'

'He's not a sore spot. He's impossible!'

'Because he writes romances?'

'Because he writes romances . . . and other things.'

'What other things?'

'Just things!'

'Such as?' Andy wasn't about to let this slide.

'Such as, he must go around seducing women in all parts of the world, just so he'll have plenty of experiences for his stories! He's a Don Juan, can't you see that?'

'If I didn't know better, I'd say you were jealous.'

'Jealous!' Tory shrieked. 'Me? Jealous? Never!'

'I'd even say you were in love with the man,' Andy went on with maddening certainty.

Tory was so angry that she forgot to watch her tongue. 'Since when are you an expert on love, marrying old Friar Richard Tuck! What does love have to do with your marriage?'

'Oh, Tory!' Andy was in tears.

Tory felt like a miserable lump. She had hurt Andy. But Andy shouldn't defend Caldwell. She didn't know what she was talking about.

Andy paid the cabbie, and they rode up in the elevator in silence.

H. Richard Merryman was in the apartment waiting for them. Andy flew into his arms sobbing. Tory went to her room and shut the door. She felt lower than low. How could she have done that? She sat on the bed and tears came to her eyes. What was wrong with her anyway? She had said a horrible thing to her best friend . . . and all because of that miserable Mitchell Caldwell. Her life had become a nightmare beyond her control, since she had met Mitchell Caldwell and allowed him into her house and . . . body.

There was a knock on the door. 'Come in,' Tory wiped her eyes.

It was H. Richard Merryman. 'I'd like to talk to you, Tory,' he said not unkindly. He took her silence as permission. 'You don't like me very much, do you?'

Tory shook her head. She might as well be truthful, she didn't have anything more to lose.

'Well now, I can't say that I blame you,' he went on. 'I'm not a dashing figure of a man,' he smiled. 'Not the sort of he-man you read about in romantic fiction. As a matter of fact, I understand that you gals have always referred to me as Friar Tuck.'

'I . . . that is, we . . .' Tory stammered.

Merryman held up his hand. 'No, wait. Let me finish. You don't have to apologise. I'm really rather flattered. If you'll remember, Friar Tuck was a pretty good fellow. Of all the names I've been called in my life, Friar Tuck far outshines them all. Now to the matter of my marrying Andy. It's true I chased her for several years, and that it was my money that first attracted her to me. She's told me that. We've been very honest with each other. But after we got to know each other, we found that we had so very much in common. We are very happy together. I love Andy, and lucky man that I am, she loves me. Didn't you see that?'

Tory was dumbfounded. Of course he was right. She had seen that. But she had been so caught up in her own interpretation, that she didn't see the truth when it was right there glowing brightly in her face.

Tears glistened in Tory's eyes. What a fool she had been. 'I am profoundly sorry,' she whispered. 'Can you ever forgive me?'

'There's nothing to forgive. You were worried about your friend Andy. You felt she was making a grave mistake. You may not have chosen the best way to tell her, but your heart was in the right place.' He smiled benevolently at her. Tory could just about believe that he was a gracious Friar Tuck at that moment.

'Come,' he held out his hand to her, 'let's go tell my bride that we have begun to be friends.'

The rest of Tory's visit went very well. She saw her publishers, thoroughly enjoyed Andy and Richard's company, and called Caldwell to say she'd be coming home on Friday.

She had wondered about talking seriously to him on the phone about their relationship and set-up, but then decided against it. It required a face-to-face meeting. Besides that, she probably should try to rethink the whole business. After all, she had been dead wrong about Andy and Richard. Maybe she wasn't being entirely fair to Caldwell. Well, we shall see, she said to herself. Tomorrow was Friday, back-to-Vermont day. Something in her felt very good about that.

Twelve

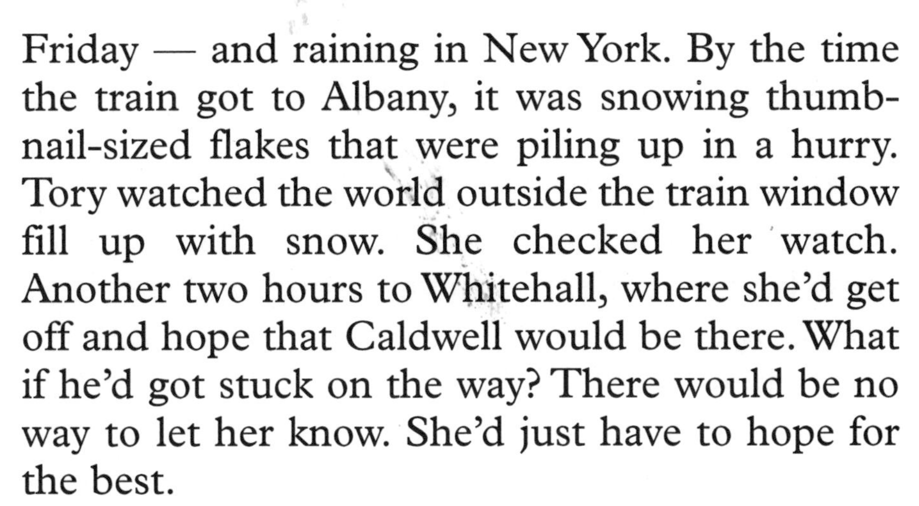

Friday — and raining in New York. By the time the train got to Albany, it was snowing thumbnail-sized flakes that were piling up in a hurry. Tory watched the world outside the train window fill up with snow. She checked her watch. Another two hours to Whitehall, where she'd get off and hope that Caldwell would be there. What if he'd got stuck on the way? There would be no way to let her know. She'd just have to hope for the best.

The train didn't seem to be in any hurry, and if anything, the storm increased as they inched their way north.

Tory was surprised and very relieved to see Caldwell waiting at the station. 'Welcome to a winter wonderland,' he grinned and reached up to give her a hand down from the train.

'Couldn't you have saved this for another day?' she smiled. He looked so good to her.

'I just wanted to stir up a little something to welcome you home,' he answered her. His hair, where it stuck out from under his hat, was sprinkled with snowflakes.

The drive back home was slow and required all Mitchell's attention. Tory sat in silence most of the way, not wanting to disturb his driving.

The hardest part of the whole trip was getting up the driveway hill. Mitchell had to make three tries at it, before the car finally inched its way up to the house.

Tory was so glad to be home. Home, she said the word in her mind again. Her snug little house was home. 'Funny,' she said out loud.

'What's that?' asked Mitchell, turning off the engine.

'It's a crazy off-beat thought, I know,' Tory answered. 'But I've never owned fifty acres of snow before. I mean, I never thought about it as *something* I owned.'

Mitchell laughed. 'Now if you could just figure out a way to harvest it.' He hopped out of the car, scooped up a snowball and lightly threw it at Tory, when she opened her door. 'You could corner the world's supply of snowballs,' he grinned.

'And I'd keep them in the woodshed,' she replied with a superior grin.

'Ouch! I'll be good, cruel landlady. See? No more snow.' He dusted the last bit off his gloves. 'Only please don't turn my poor woodshed into a giant refrigerator.'

'Nobody messes with the Queen's snow,' she replied, and grabbed a handful off the bonnet of the car. Her snowball landed right in the middle of Mitchell's jacket.

'In that case . . .' They were soon winging snowballs back and forth at each other over the bonnet of the car. Most of Mitchell's body shots were hitting. Tory threw wild. Then just as Mitchell was getting up from leaning over to grab another handful, one of hers splattered right into his neck.

'Oh ho!' he laughed. 'You shall pay for that one!' He came roaring around the car. Tory was laughing so hard that she only was able to run a few yards before he caught up with her. He held her fast with one arm and Tory was sure he intended to wash her face with snow. She was very surprised when he kissed her instead. He drew back and took a long breath. 'One kiss, that's the penalty for one snowball down the neck.' He held her out at arm's length and looked at her critically. 'One kiss for one snowball,' he repeated in mock seriousness. 'I guess it was worth it.'

'Worth it?' she spluttered.

He frowned. 'Maybe I was wrong. Let me try again.'

Tory started to splutter, but before she could get any word out, he had covered her mouth with another kiss. She struggled momentarily, then let herself be swept away by the passionate insistence of his lips. What's the harm in a little kiss, she told herself.

Mitchell pulled away with difficulty. 'Tory?'

'Hmm?' she smiled up at him. There were tiny

perfect snowflakes caught in his eyelashes. He could have been a magic prince from some enchanted land.

'Let's go inside, Tory,' he whispered in her ear.

She nodded her head, afraid to speak and break the spell.

Mitchell took her hand and they walked into the house. Tory was surprised to see that the table was carefully set for two. There were candles, a bottle of wine and a fresh loaf of bread. A single red rose was in a bud-vase in the middle of the table.

'What's this?' she asked.

'A welcome-home dinner,' he answered. He squeezed her hand. 'Shall we start with dessert?'

She nodded, and followed him into her bedroom. The little voice inside her head finally made itself heard. What are you doing?

I'm doing what I want to do, she answered herself.

Come what may?

Yes, whatever comes I will handle it. Right now, I need this. Go away. I'm not listening.

Okay, but don't say I didn't warn you.

They stood a little way apart and began to take off their clothes. Mitchell's eyes devoured Tory's well proportioned body. When she got down to her bra and panties, he asked: 'Would you like some help?'

She smiled her answer. Her body was crying out to have him touch it. The feel of his fingers on her skin sent delicious tingles up and down her spine. He cupped her breasts gently in his hands. He bent his head to kiss the swelling skin on the top of each mound. 'I think they want out, don't they?'

'Yes,' she whispered.

He unhooked her bra and let her breasts hang free. The nipples were pink and puckered with delight. 'Oh Tory,' he moaned. Ever so gently he again cupped each pink melon. He traced the outline of each nipple with his thumb. Then he gave first one and then the other a generous kiss.

Tory was almost beside herself with desire. She could feel the red-hot flame of passion burning brighter and brighter, climbing up her thighs, enveloping her whole body in a fever of desire.

When Mitchell stood up, she could see that he was as aroused as she. He leaned forward to kiss her lips again. She put her arms around his neck, lightly kneading the back of his neck. He hooked his thumbs inside her panties and slid them lower and lower. As he went lower with his hands, his lips travelled lower and lower too. Down to her chin, her throat, her chest and her belly. Tory was in a delirium of want and needing. Mitchell kissed her until she could stand it no longer.

'Mitchell, Mitchell,' she moaned.

'Do you want me, Tory?'

'Yes, yes, I want you.' Her whisper was full of the heat of her body.

He picked her up and gently laid her on the bed. 'You're so lovely. I want to start at the top again.' He kissed her lips then trailed down her body once again with little kisses and playful nips that increased Tory's desire to the very brink. 'Please, please,' she begged.

Mitchell spread her thighs and she guided him to the seat of passion.

Together they swayed, locked in the rhythm of their swelling need for each other. Two bodies as one ship riding higher and higher as the waves come on and on, rising to cresting height as they near the shore. Then suddenly breaking through with the thunder and power of release sounding through their bodies. Everything caught in the sweeping majesty of the roller as it comes melting up the beach to leave its mark on the sand.

They both felt like surfers who had expended the last shred of energy riding the waves. They lay side by side on the bed, enjoying the fulfilment of a ride well won.

After a little while, Mitchell broke the silence. 'Tory?'

'Yes?'

'I'm glad you're home.'

'And I'm glad to be here.' There was in her the wild hope that he was going to say I love you, but she knew that was all it was — a wild hope. Why does it matter to you, the little voice in her head said. You said you could handle this. You'd better! it warned. If he loved me, then I could be free to decide whether or not to love him, she explained to herself. But since he doesn't, then I haven't that option. So see, I couldn't possibly love him.

And I don't . . . or won't . . . or whatever. She dismissed her voice of conscience by intently studying the pattern on the wallpaper.

Mitchell sat up and stretched. Even after the loving, the look of him sent warm feelings through her body. 'Now, how would you like some chicken tetrazzini, dear landlady?' He lightly touched the tip of her nose. She looked cross-eyed at his finger. 'It's highly recommended for cross-eyed lovers,' he grinned.

'In that case I'd better have some,' she answered. He had used the word 'lovers'. Well, that's what they were, weren't they? Lovers. They were some other unprintable words too. To be a lover did not necessarily mean one was in love, she reminded herself hastily.

The tetrazzini was delicious. And the fresh bread was perfect, yeasty and tasty. Tory lifted her wineglass in salute. 'My compliments to the chef. If I could afford you, I'd hire you.'

A mischievous glint sparkled in Mitchell's eyes. 'Just what would you hire me for?'

'For your expertise in the kitchen, of course,' she answered.

Mitchell looked thoughtful. 'I don't believe I've ever done it in the kitchen,' he joked.

'I was referring to your culinary skills,' she retorted. Then taking the bull by the horns, she continued: 'But since we're on the subject, you seem to have done it, as you say, in just about every other corner of the world.' There, let him cleverly squirm out of that one.

'Oh?'

'Yes,' she went on, 'I happened to pick up a few of your books while I was in New York. Paris, Jamaica, New York, and I suspect that there are other scenes of conquest as well. You certainly get around. A girl in every port, so to speak.'

'Is that what you think of me?'

'I didn't say what I thought, only what I read,' she answered.

'You aren't one of those people who believe everything they read, are you? You're too intelligent for that.'

'Well,' she sniffed, 'I think the point here is not my intelligence, but the depth of your research.'

'Oh ho,' he laughed, but his eyes were mirthless. 'I can't believe you're serious.'

Tory didn't reply, but continued to regard him with a steady gaze.

Mitchell pushed back his chair and slumped comfortably, hands in his pockets. He seemed to be considering his answer. 'I'll admit to having been in New York, Paris, Jamaica and even in England and Ireland. You'll find, if you ever decide to read further, that I've used England and Ireland in my writing too. I've also set stories in any number of countries I've never had the good fortune to visit. Writers do that, you know. It's a perfectly acceptable practice. If you do your homework, which means a lot of reading on the subject, you can almost believe yourself that you've been to Seattle or Singapore, even if you've never set foot there. And as far as the girl in every port goes,' he shifted uncomfortably.

Here comes the good part, Tory thought.

'Human anatomy is the same the world over. We all make love in basically the same way. I don't have to make love in thirty-seven languages to know how it's done, or to write about it convincingly. All I have to know is what pleases one man and one woman. If I understand that, then I can write about it over and over again, given the variations that are a part of any loving relationship.'

He made it sound so cut and dried. But he hadn't, Tory noted, denied having had a girl in every port. He only said it wasn't necessary.

'There,' he smiled, 'have I answered all your questions?'

'For now,' she answered.

Mitchell got up and began to clear the table. Tory got up to help. 'No, you sit still,' he told her. 'Tonight is my treat.'

She couldn't help wondering if their love-making was part of his treat. He seemed to be able to take it all so lightly. She wished she could do that. Well, she was either going to learn — or quit.

Mitchell was filling the sink with hot soapy water. He had his back to her. 'As long as we're on the subject . . .' he paused. 'Don't you think we should talk about our relationship? We don't want it to get out of hand.'

She nodded, forgetting that he couldn't see her. He turned around to see if she was listening, when she didn't answer.

'Y . . . yes,' she stammered. She was dreading it. It was so much nicer to hold on to some hope, to imagine that maybe they could have a loving relationship that would be free to grow. Did they have to draw lines around it? Did they really have to say here are the rules? Was it necessary to say that no little sparks of love would be allowed to grow? That this was only an intimate relationship to please the body, never the heart? Fresh from their lovemaking, with the feel of Mitchell's body still on hers, Tory found it very difficult to think in business like terms. 'You're right,' she suppressed a sigh, 'we need some rules.'

'Good.' He was nodding his head over the dishpan. He seemed to be waiting for her to begin.

'First of all, I think it's important that we both understand that I live in the house and you live in the woodshed — with the exception of the kitchen and the bath, and that neither of us is to trespass.'

'Agreed . . . go on.'

'I think we should agree that no matter what sort of . . .' Tory cleared her throat, 'intimate relationship we have, we have no strings on each other.' There was a part of Tory that wanted to scream at that.

'Very good.' Mitchell turned around and added: 'And nobody's going to get bent out of shape if either of us brings home a person of the opposite sex.' He studied her face intently.

'Of course not,' she answered, and wanted to

choke on the words. Somewhere way back in her mind a little voice was asking — why are you agreeing to this?

'Have we covered everything?' Mitchell was drying his hands.

'I think so,' Tory answered.

'Good. Then let's shake on it, shall we?' He smiled.

Tory reached out and shook his hands gingerly. The feel of his strong hand wrapped around hers was still doing things to her inside. Damn. And why did he have to have such soulful eyes?

Mitchell snapped his fingers. 'Hey, I just remembered you haven't met the newest member of our family yet. Our . . . I mean, your new furnace!'

Mitchell led the way to the cellar. There, sitting on the concrete slab, was a very small bright furnace. 'There she is, isn't she a beauty!'

'It's so small,' Tory raised her eyebrows. 'Are you sure it's large enough to heat this house?'

'The new furnaces are only one quarter of the size of the old ones,' Mitchell explained. 'But they're much more efficient.'

'What did you do with the beast?' Tory peered around in the dark corners of the basement, half expecting to see the ancient beastly furnace lurking in the shadows.

'The plumber took it away — in pieces. I tell you, I was never so happy to see anything dismantled as that old pile of iron and troubles.'

Tory smiled at his description. 'How much?' She might as well get it over with.

Mitchell named a price that was well over a thousand dollars.

Tory gulped.

'Looks like you'll be having me around in the woodshed for longer than you planned.' He looked at her stricken face. 'Cheer up. I'm very good at following rules. You'll hardly know I'm here.'

There was no way she could tell him that she was worried about how she would handle those rules that they had both so blithely agreed to not five minutes ago.

When they returned upstairs, the clock on the kitchen shelf was chiming seven. 'Time for me to be trudging home,' Mitchell quipped. He opened the woodshed door. Cold air came pouring out. 'My fire must have gone out. Night, landlady,' he tipped an imaginary hat and shut the door. Tory didn't envy him having to live in a room with a woodstove that could go out. But that was his problem. It was his idea. He wanted to do it. Still it made her feel a little guilty to have such a nice toasty house just the other side of the door . . . especially since he had been the one who bought the furnace. But given their agreement, she couldn't think of any way to share her heat without putting them both in jeopardy. Maybe it was possible to run a heat line out to the woodshed. She would ask him tomorrow.

Tory unpacked her bag and put her clothes

away. Her bed with its tossed and tumbled bedclothes bothered her. She straightened it. No sense thinking about what had gone on in those sheets and blankets several hours ago. It was fun. She enjoyed it. But it was over and no sense brooding about it.

Several hours later, when she went to bed, she hoped she'd fall right to sleep. She didn't want to think about Mitchell Caldwell in her bed. She'd think about Andy and Richard instead. But thinking about Andy and Richard made her think about love. And thinking about love got her right back to Mitchell Caldwell.

That's what I was afraid of, said the little voice in her head.

Thirteen

Caldwell good-naturedly agreed that it was a splendid idea to put a heat zone from the furnace out into the woodshed. He even raised his own rent to reflect the money and time he'd save not having to cut and burn wood to keep warm.

Now that the house stayed evenly warm all day and all night, they seemed to see each other less and less. There was no longer a cranky beast to complain about or wring hands over. And each had a January deadline to meet — Caldwell on a book, and Tory on an illustration assignment for a children's picture-book. It was a new client, and she was most anxious to have everything done correctly and on time.

Christmas was coming. Tory had no close family to celebrate with, and Mitchell's sister Sally and her family were going to the Virgin Islands for the holidays. Caldwell had off-handedly volunteered the information a couple of days before Christmas.

'They asked me to come too,' he said. He was

bent over in front of the refrigerator. 'And,' he stood up with a jar of olives in hand, 'much as I'd like to partake of some sun and sand, I told them I couldn't. Can't afford the time away from my typewriter, you know.'

Tory was sitting at the kitchen table with a bologna sandwich. She nodded with her mouthful. When she didn't answer him, he looked sideways at her. She pointed to her mouth.

He smiled in understanding. 'You going anywhere?' he asked.

She shook her head, no.

'Well then, shall we have a little get-together here for the two of us to celebrate the day?'

She swallowed her mouthful. 'That would be nice,' she agreed.

Tory bought candy canes and a good bottle of wine. If the truth be known, she couldn't bear to ignore Christmas altogether. She bought a wreath for the door and a tiny ceramic angel to hang from the ceiling lamp in the kitchen.

Caldwell left early in the morning on Christmas Eve. Tory heard the kitchen door shut and his car leave the yard. By the time he returned, the bleak December sun had set. He came into the kitchen with cheeks as red as apples and his arms full of packages.

Tory just happened to be in the kitchen when he came in. She had just been peering down the dark hill, looking for his lights. He had been gone so long, she was getting worried. But of course she didn't tell him that.

'Ho, ho, ho, Santa Claus has arrived!' She laughed merrily and shut the door behind him. 'Let me guess, you've been to the North Pole?'

'Ah ah ah.' He put his packages on the table and shook a still gloved finger at her. 'Mustn't ask questions at Christmas time. Christmas is for surprises!' With that, he picked up most of his packages and marched off into the woodshed.

The next day, Christmas Day, they made a nice roast goose, taking time to fuss and sip the good rich wine Tory had provided. Caldwell had bought candlesticks and a tiny tree for the centre of the table. The little tree's pea-sized ornaments glinted and winked in the candlelight.

When they finished eating, Caldwell pulled a long box from behind the woodshed door. It was wrapped in glossy white paper with pink and lace ribbons. 'For you, my dear landlady.'

'Oh no,' said Tory, her skin flushed from the wine. 'We didn't say anything about presents. I didn't get you anything,' she added in dismay.

'This is just a simple thank-you gift from renter to rentee,' he smiled warmly. 'Nothing more.'

'Looks awfully fancy for something simple,' Tory replied.

'Don't judge a book by its cover, nor a package by its wrappings,' Caldwell intoned.

Tory opened the elegant box. The pink tissue paper inside was folded over and held together with a golden seal. Tory carefully tore the tissue paper to keep the seal intact. Under the paper was a soft blue cashmere robe. 'Ohh . . . you shouldn't have . . . it's so soft. Something simple? You call this something simple?'

'It's the colour of your eyes. I couldn't resist it,' he answered.

A part of her thought she should make him take it back. What was he buying? Or what did he think he was buying? But one look at his soft, kind eyes, and she knew it was all right to accept the gift. 'Thank you, thank you,' she said graciously.

'You're very welcome. My pleasure!' he beamed.

Christmas Day ended on a warm note. They wished each other much cheer and drank the last of the wine.

'I enjoyed our merry little Christmas,' Caldwell said almost shyly.

'Me too,' Tory agreed.

He looked as though he wanted very much to reach over and touch her, to carry her off to his den, but the idea faded. She saw caution come into his eyes.

'Well,' she looked down nervously, 'I just want to thank you again for my lovely robe . . .'

'That's fine, that's fine . . .' He, too, looked away, then got up from the table. He bowed graciously and saluted her with a sad little smile. 'A very merry Christmas to you, my dear landlady.' Then, he walked into the woodshed without looking back and shut the door quietly.

Tory fingered the soft cashmere and watched

the blue of the material seem to run like wet watercolour, as her eyes filled with tears. 'Oh my,' she said quietly to herself.

Oh my, indeed, said the little voice inside her head.

Christmas was no sooner over than it was time for Andy's wedding. When Tory got to New York, she was quickly swept into preparations for the wedding. There were all sorts of last-minute details to help with. Andy was positively frantic to have everything go well.

Richard took Tory aside and confided that he was worried about Andy. Wasn't Andy too worried? Wasn't she making too big a production out of a small wedding? And would he have his sweet Andy, when all was said and done, or a frayed exhausted woman? He was as frantic as Andy was, but about Andy rather than about the wedding.

Tory did her best to calm them both. She had little time to think about her own troubles — or troubles of her own making, she told herself bluntly.

The day before the wedding everything seemed to fall into place. There didn't seem to be anything to do except go to the rehearsal and rehearsal dinner in the evening. Tory was sitting in a chair in Andy's apartment. Andy was pacing. Even though she couldn't think of anything she had to do, she was certain she had forgotten something.

'I know I should save my breath,' Tory began, 'but for heaven's sake Andy calm down. It's all ready. You've thought of everything. Everything is done. You owe it to Richard to be a beautiful serene bride, and you'll never be that if you don't give yourself a rest.'

'I know, I know.' Andy was wringing her hands. 'You're right.' She went over and perched on the edge of a chair. She tapped her feet on the floor.

'Sit back,' Tory instructed. 'I've never seen anyone less relaxed sitting in a chair than you are.'

Andy sat back in the chair. She wiggled and twisted. She drummed her fingers on the chair's arm. 'I'm relaxed. I'm relaxed.'

'Couldn't prove it to me,' Tory smiled at her friend.

'Just you wait until it's your turn,' Andy replied. 'Then you'll know what I'm going through. Brides are entitled to the jitters.'

'If you say so,' Tory answered.

'Just you wait,' Andy repeated.

'It will be a long wait,' Tory answered.

'Now Tory, you mustn't let one bitter experience sour you forever. Adam was a first-class stinker, but he's only one of many fish in the ocean.'

'If you say so,' Tory answered again. She didn't particularly relish talking about Adam. But Andy had calmed down a bit, now that she wasn't caught up in her own worries about the wedding. She could stand to discuss Adam if it meant distracting Andy for a while.

'That's your problem, you know,' Andy went

on. 'You get so involved with one thought or one person, that you can't see anything else. You're really too loyal for your own good. Though, I must say I'm certainly happy to have you as a loyal friend. I mean, look at how you held on to your dream about a place in Vermont. I don't know anyone else who would have gone through what you did just to make their dream come true. But you're doing the same thing about that rotten Adam. He's gone, and good riddance. You have to let go. You have to go on. And you can't let one bad experience ruin the whole of the rest of your life.'

How about two, Tory was thinking to herself, though she didn't say anything.

'As I said, there are lots of other fish in the ocean.' Andy continued talking and Tory, in spite of her good intentions, stopped listening.

'Tory?' Andy was leaning forward, giving her friend a quizzical look.

'What?'

'I asked you a question. I guess you weren't listening.'

'Oh, I'm sorry,' Tory replied. 'What did you ask?'

'I was asking about your lodger, what's his name — Valerie Valentine to the world,' Andy giggled.

'He's fine, just fine.'

'Oh?' Andy was now regarding Tory closely. 'You see much of him?'

'No, not much. We're both very busy. Not

much different from living in a flat. We seldom see each other.' Tory tried to dismiss the subject of Mitchell Caldwell as quickly as possible.

Andy was drumming her fingers again. 'Have a nice Christmas?'

'Fine.'

'What did you do? Did you go anywhere?'

'No, I stayed home.'

'Just stayed home? Isn't that rather boring?'

'No, it wasn't boring. We had a real sweet old-fashioned Christmas.'

'We?' Andy asked.

Tory wanted to put the word back in her mouth. 'We,' she answered, 'my lodger and I.'

'You and your lodger spent Christmas together?' A sly smile was spreading across Andy's face.

'Yes, that's correct,' Tory answered very precisely.

'Okay.' Andy got right down to brass tacks. 'You are a terrible liar, Tory Higgins, and you don't hide things well either. You might as well tell me what's going on between you and . . . what is his name? I can't go on calling him Valerie Valentine.'

Tory sighed. 'His name is Mitchell Caldwell.' She paused.

'Go on,' Andy prompted.

'He's very nice looking. He's kind, gentle, funny, sexy and a super lover.'

'Wheet!' Andy whistled.

'But he's also not interested in any sort of permanent relationship.'

'That's easy, change his mind.'

'It's not easy. I wish I could.'

'You forgot to add one other thing,' Andy added wisely. 'You're in love with him.'

'No!' Tory said with more heat than she intended.

'You can tell me "no" till the cows come home,' Andy replied evenly. 'The fact is that you are. It's written all over you. If I hadn't been so busy with this wedding, I would have seen it long ago.'

'Is it really that plain?' Tory asked morosely.

'It certainly is.' Andy nodded her pretty head. 'Now, the problem is, what are you going to do about it?'

'Probably nothing.'

'Probably nothing!' Andy shrieked. 'Victoria Higgins, how can you of all people say that? Never-give-up Tory Higgins is giving up? I never thought I'd live to see the day! I'm shocked! I am!'

Tory had to smile at her dramatic friend. 'Okay, then, if I'm not supposed to give up, then tell me what I'm supposed to do.'

'Fight for him, of course!' Andy made a fist and pounded on the chair-arm.

'But how?'

'Well . . . well, first of all I'd tell him . . . I'll bet you haven't told him you love him, have you?'

'No. . .but. . .'

'No buts. How's he supposed to know you love him?'

'You just said it was written all over me. And he's certainly seen all over me,' she added with a smirk.

'What a man can read and what a woman can read are two different things.' Andy shook her head. 'I can see you have a lot to learn. You go back to Vermont, Victoria,' Andy pointed a finger at Tory, 'and you tell that man that you love him.'

'And if I don't?'

'You'll probably lose him.'

'I told Adam I loved him, and I lost him,' Tory replied.

'No great loss.' Tory winced. 'Is that true or not?' Andy demanded.

'It's true,' Tory replied weakly. 'Only it took me a long time to figure it out. Maybe I'm wrong about Mitchell too.'

'Maybe,' Andy allowed. 'Then that too will be no great loss.'

'Ouch!' Tory responded. 'This is my heart and life you're so blithely tossing around.'

'We are speaking nitty-gritty here, Tory. Only good friends can do that. Life isn't easy. You can get hurt. But some things are worth risking, just as some things are worth saving for. Besides that,' Andy waved all Tory's objections aside, 'I can't believe that Valerie Valentine, alias Mitchell Caldwell, isn't worth risking something for. I just know in my heart that he's pretty nearly perfect. He couldn't have written so many heartfelt romances if he wasn't mighty special.'

Tory didn't say a word. Her mind was awhirl. What if Andy was right?

'Well?'

'Well what?'

'Are you going to do it, or not?'

'I'm thinking about it.'

'Forget the thinking about it. I'm sure you've already done more than enough of that. Just do it!' Andy raised both her fists above her head and shook them at Tory. 'Okay?'

'Maybe,' Tory answered tentatively.

'Just maybe? I guarantee results!'

'Oh Andy.' Tory laughed and patted her friend on the knee. 'There would be results all right. But they might not be the right results.'

Andy shook her head in despair. 'You're impossible. We should have arranged marriages in this country. That way, I could call up your Mitchell and fix the whole situation.'

'You wouldn't!'

'I might.' Andy narrowed her eyes.

'Promise me, you've got to promise me, you won't do any meddling.'

'Then, you've got to promise me that you will do something,' Andy finished triumphantly.

'All right, I'll do something,' Tory promised.

'Good. That's all set.' Andy beamed.

Later, when Richard came in, Andy went sailing up to him. 'Guess what?'

'What, my love?'

'Tory's going to be the next one married!'

'Oh, Andy!' Tory moaned.

'That's wonderful!' Richard gave his bride a hug. 'Who's the lucky guy? And are we invited?'

Tory patiently tried to explain. When she was done, Richard gave Andy a kiss. 'Don't sell my little bride short, Tory. She's mighty sharp in the heart department!'

Fourteen

The wedding was beautiful. Andy was a lovely bride. Everything was perfect, the flowers, the music, the setting and the food. Anyone looking at the bride and groom could see that they were very much in love. It may be satins and lace, Caldwell, Tory was thinking to herself, but it's also something very special. There's something basically right and good, and soul-satisfying about a man and woman standing up before their friends and relatives, and pledging their love and commitment to each other. And you, Caldwell, can't change that.

Tory kept running the idea over and over in her mind of telling Mitchell that she loved him. What would he say? He'd probably remind her that he wasn't having anything to do with a steady-couple relationship. The only hearts and flowers he believed in took place between the pages of his books. But then again . . . what if he had changed his mind? Should she risk it? Was it worth it? Certainly, she could stand it if he should say 'yes' he loved her too. But could she stand to hear him say no? It would be too humiliating. It would hurt too much. But then again, could she live with the thought that she never gave it a chance? No matter how many different ways she approached the subject, she could come to no definite conclusion one way or another.

After the reception, the brand-new Mr and Mrs H. Richard Merryman left amid clouds of rose petals and good wishes for their honeymoon. They were going to Tahiti. The South Pacific. It sounded so exotic and sun-drenched, so warm and inviting compared to January in New York.

Tory wrapped her coat more tightly around her, and walked the few blocks to Andy's apartment. Andy had insisted that she use the apartment when they were away.

'You can stay as long as you like. Consider it yours. You might even want to invite Mitchell down to share it with you!' Tory blushed at the suggestion.

'He wouldn't come.'

Andy raised her eyebrows. 'Did you ask him?'

Tory had to admit that she hadn't ever asked Mitchell Caldwell anything like that. But still, she was quite certain that he wouldn't dream of coming to New York to share an apartment with Tory Higgins.

Tory spent the next day, which was Sunday, padding around the apartment in her robe and slippers. She made a huge pot of coffee, had some orange juice and bagels with cream cheese, and read *The New York Times.* It was such a luxury to spend hours poring over the paper. She knew if she were back in Vermont, the thought of unfinished work would have got her back to the drawing-board. She was beginning to see quite clearly that her years of diligent work, striving to make her dream come true, had turned her into a workaholic. Now that she had accomplished it, she didn't have to work quite so hard. She could relax a little. It was fun to spend the whole day reading. She could do that now; it was just a matter of giving herself permission.

Such as? The little voice in her head asked.

Such as, exactly what I'm doing, she answered.

Thinking of Mitchell Caldwell? The little voice snickered.

'Some voice of conscience you are,' Tory said out loud. 'You're supposed to be on my side, I thought.'

I am, more than you know, the voice went on.

'Some fine mess this is.' Tory shook her head. 'Here I am arguing with my own conscience about Mitchell Caldwell.'

No matter what she did, thoughts of Mitchell Caldwell came rolling into her mind.

Half way through the afternoon, she got dressed. A weak winter's sun was trying without much success to warm things up. Tory took a brisk walk up Fifth Avenue. A gusty January wind was blowing. Her scarf trailed out behind her like a banner on a pole. Tears stung her eyes, partly from the wind, and partly because the thought of loving Caldwell made her very unhappy.

She stopped and had an early dinner at a small Chinese restaurant. The Moo Shu Pork was excellent, but half the time Tory wasn't tasting it. For all the attention she was paying to what was in her mouth, it could have been cardboard.

Tomorrow she would see the publishers and Tuesday, she would go home. Home to Vermont and Mitchell Caldwell. And to tell him . . . ? Would she? Could she? And what was more important, should she?

Back in the apartment Tory kept eyeing the telephone. She had to call Caldwell to tell him what train to meet. Several times she reached for the phone, then stopped in mid-air. This is really silly, she told herself. But still, she couldn't bring herself to dial. It's a simple matter of conveying one message — the train will arrive at three, she told herself. Anyone with the power of speech can do it. Why am I so hysterical about one simple phone call? I want to hear his voice. I long to hear his voice . . . and yet, I'm afraid.

That was what it boiled down to, of course. She was afraid. Just knowing that she might, when she got back to Vermont, say 'I love you' to Caldwell, made her afraid to say anything to him. It didn't make a whole lot of sense, but that's the way it was.

She finally talked herself into waiting until tomorrow to make the call. I'll be calmer tomorrow, she assured herself.

She spent a restless night. She told herself that was because she was alone in this great big plush apartment in New York City. She told herself she wasn't used to the muffled sounds of traffic that went on all night. But in her heart of hearts, she knew it had to do with someone who lived three hundred miles from there.

The next day she saw her publishers. They were very pleased with her work. She went away from the meeting glowing with the praise they had heaped on her head. They had also given her another assignment. Being in love with Caldwell certainly hadn't affected her work. Maybe it had made it better. That was a disturbing thought. If if was better with Caldwell in her life, then what would happen if he left?

She unlocked the door to Andy's apartment. The time had come. No further excuses. Having at last made up her mind to do it, she didn't even take off her coat. She punched the numbers and listened to the tuneless melody that played in her ear. It took a moment for the circuits to clear, then it rang. She could see the phone on the kitchen counter. She could see Caldwell coming out of the woodshed to answer it. She could imagine his hand reaching out to pick up the receiver.

'Hello?' said a strange voice.

'Hello,' Tory replied. She must have punched the wrong numbers. This was a female voice, no mistake about that. 'Oh, I must have a wrong number . . .' Tory began.

'Not necessarily,' the voice laughed musically.

'I'm calling Mitchell Caldwell,' Tory said.

'He's not . . .'

'What?' Tory asked; she had begun to talk at the same time as the other person, and had missed what was said.

'I said,' the voice repeated, 'that Mitch isn't here right now. Can I take a message?'

'Oh!' Tory answered. Who was this female person in her house?

'Is there any message?' the voice asked again.

'Who is that?' Tory demanded. She wasn't usually so curt and rude, but calling and finding a strange female voice answering the phone in her house was more than she could take at the moment.

'And who is that?' the voice asked, equally rudely.

'This,' Tory retorted pointedly, 'is Tory Higgins. And for your information, you are in *my* house!'

'Oh, Tory Higgins,' laughed the voice. 'Mitch said you might call. What can I do for you?'

Tory was very tempted to say, get out of my house, but she didn't. 'Please tell Mr Caldwell that my train will be getting in at three tomorrow.'

'Three tomorrow,' the voice repeated. 'I'll tell him. Is there anything else?' The voice was bitingly sweet.

'No,' Tory answered between clenched teeth. She let the phone clatter into its cradle without saying another word.

So, that was it, was it? While the cat's away the mouse will play! To think that she had been agonising over telling Mitchell Caldwell that she loved him! How dare he have a woman in *her* house! How dare he! For all she knew they probably had made love in her bed! Tears welled up in her eyes and spilled over. She had half a mind to call back and tell whoever she was to tell Mitchell Caldwell to be gone before she got there. She wasn't going to have him and his . . . his . . . his tart in *her* house! But no, that wasn't good enough. She wanted to be able to tell him herself! Besides that, she still needed a lift home from the station. Let him pick her up and take her home. He owed her that. And then, she'd throw him out!

Needless to say, Tory went to bed and got about ten minutes of sleep. She dragged herself out of bed in the grey dawn, red-eyed and groggy. It didn't take her long to straighten up the room and pack her bag. She didn't eat anything. It probably wouldn't have stayed down anyway, the way she was feeling.

She bought an extra cup of coffee at the station, then she boarded the train. She kept checking her watch. The train was five minutes late getting started, and it seemed like hours. Tory watched the towns and villages along the Hudson River slip by the train window. The sky was full of clouds. They looked like old cake batter spilled across the sky. Everything looked bleak and bare and dreary. Tory was quite satisfied with the feel of the world today. It matched her mood precisely.

The conductor was a jolly fellow, who was joshing with the passengers. When he walked by Tory, she shut her eyes and pretended to sleep. She didn't want anyone trying to jolly her up.

After Albany, the sky got heavier and darker. It suited Tory just fine. She watched the little New York villages pass by. She looked at the houses and tried to imagine families in them. Were there really people who loved each other under those roofs? Or were they all pretending? Surely, there were some happy couples in the world, weren't there? Or was it just one gigantic farce? Or was she just one of the unlucky ones?

The train slowed and stopped. Fort Edward. The next stop was Whitehall, where Caldwell would be waiting for her. In spite of herself, she felt the muscles in her thighs tighten. She looked down at herself in disgust. Traitors! Caldwell is over and done with. No more of that. Tears threatened to spill over. She willed them back down.

Clack, clack, clack went the wheels over the rails. Done, done, done Tory repeated to herself.

Finally the train slowed again. Tory got her bag down from the overhead rack and picked up her illustration case. Before the train came to a stop, she was at the back of the car, ready to get out.

'In a hurry?' the conductor grinned at her. 'You'll be sorry. It's mighty awful cold out there!'

Tory just nodded her head and gave him a weak smile.

Caldwell was there waiting. For a moment she had the fear that he might not be alone. She glanced over at the car. It was empty.

'Welcome home, landlady.' Caldwell grinned at her in his easy manner. 'Did you enjoy your stay in the big city?' He had taken her luggage and was walking a little ahead of her. He turned to look at her when she didn't answer. 'Oh, oh, red eyes!' he laughed. 'Must have been some celebration! You look a little hungover, if you don't mind my saying so.'

'For your information Mr Caldwell, the wedding was beautiful! Something you, naturally, wouldn't appreciate, and I am *not hungover!*'

'Oh touchy, touchy,' he chuckled.

How could he be so easy-going and cheerful? Didn't he have any idea that she might be very angry at him? Was he so self-centred and self-indulgent, that he had no inkling of the bomb that was about to fall on him?

'Let's see,' he continued in his jovial mood. 'You'll want to hear how your house fared while you were away. I'm happy to report that the new blue furnace has continued to behave perfectly. You got several books and several bills in the mail. There was also one postcard from someone named Bettie. She's in Bermuda with Don . . . or was that Dan? She says it's a pastel island and that she'll write you a proper letter when she gets back. I always read other people's postcards,' he chuckled. 'Oh, and I finished up the quart of milk you left in the fridge. I figured it would be sour before you got back. I guess that's about all. I don't think I forgot anything.'

'How about the sweet young thing who answered the phone?' Tory asked. She hadn't meant it to sound so . . . so jealous. But there it was, that was the way it came out.

'Lisa?'

'That's her name — Lisa? I asked her name on the phone and she wouldn't give it to me,' Tory replied icily.

Mitchell raised his eyebrows and gave her a quick look. 'Her name is Lisa Adams,' he continued. 'She said you were . . . ahem . . . shall we say, a little rude on the phone.'

'I was *rude*?' Tory squawked. 'I call up and find a strange woman in my house, and she says I was rude? What was she doing in my house? And where were you?'

'She was answering the phone for me, since I was expecting you to call. And I had gone to the store — if that's any of your business.'

'What goes on in my house is certainly my business!'

'I wasn't aware that you had to okay my visitors,' he replied drily.

'I don't intend to have your so-called friends dancing around in my house and being rude on my phone!'

'But it's okay for you to be rude?'

'I can do what I want in my house! You cannot have your tarts in my house!'

'Is that what you think of me?'

'If the shoe fits, Caldwell, you'd jolly well better put it on and wear it!' She was so angry and hurt all at once, that the tears she had so far held back now came rolling down her face. She turned to look out of the car window so that Caldwell couldn't see. She'd be damned if she'd let him see her cry over him.

They were both silent for some time. Finally Mitchell spoke. 'What do you want, Tory?'

'I want you to leave,' she said almost in a whisper.

'All right.' He paused. 'You're probably right. It's not going to work. We both need peace and quiet, and we're not going to get it if there's a war going on between us.'

To hear him speak of leaving made Tory's insides turn upside down. But it was better for him to go now. It could only get worse, she told herself. She certainly wouldn't be able to stand seeing another woman going in and out of the woodshed. No, it was far better that he left while she still had some shreds of her heart intact.

'If this storms holds off, I may be able to leave tomorrow,' he continued evenly and seemingly without emotion.

At the mention of the word tomorrow, Tory felt as though she had been stabbed. Tomorrow!

How quickly everything changes. He would be gone tomorrow!

'If not,' Mitchell went on, 'it may not be for a day or two. Is that satisfactory?'

'Yes,' she replied in a tight small voice. She was glad she didn't have to say anything more. She was having a hard time keeping her emotions in check.

When they got in the house, Tory saw that the table was set for two. Another welcome-home dinner, no doubt. She went straight to her room. She could hear him putting the dishes away, then she heard the door to the woodshed open and close.

Tory had tea and toast and went to bed early. The quicker tomorrow came and went, the better. She tossed and turned all night.

Fifteen

The next morning was still heavy with grey threatening skies, but nothing had let loose yet. Tory heard a car come up the drive. She looked out. It was a pickup. She could hear voices out in the woodshed. Someone was helping Mitchell pack.

By lunchtime the pickup had made two trips down the drive piled with Mitchell's furnishings. She wondered where he had found to go so quickly. Probably Lisa was taking him in . . . away from this rude landlady.

Suddenly she remembered the furnace. She still owed Mitchell for the furnace! She went to the woodshed door and knocked.

'Come in,' Mitchell called out.

She stood in the doorway and surveyed the almost empty room. 'I just wanted you to know that I will pay you for the furnace. If you'll tell me where I can reach you, I'll send you a cheque once a month until it's paid off.'

'Thank you, I appreciate that.' He was very,

very serious. 'Since I'm not sure where I'll be permanently, you can send the cheque to General Delivery at the post office. They'll know where to reach me.'

Tory simply nodded her head. She wasn't even going to know where he was! He would just walk out of here, out of her life, and that would be it! She turned and shut the door before the tears began to roll down her face.

The pickup came back one more time. It didn't take long before both the pickup and Mitchell's car started down the driveway. It was just then that the snow began to fall.

Tory sat over her drawing-board and let the tears fall until there were no more. She strained her ears to hear if they might come back. Maybe something had been forgotten. She waited and listened a long time, but all continued to be completely silent. The world seemed to be filling up with silence.

That night she fell into an exhausted sleep with terrible dreams. The world was empty of people. Everywhere she went, she was alone. Even in the centre of New York York City, there were no cars, no buses, no taxis and not one person.

When she awoke in the early morning, it was still snowing. She stared out at the alien white world. 'Now is the winter of our discontent' — the line from Shakespeare ran through her head. She couldn't remember the play it was from. Watching the world fill up with snow made her feel utterly alone. It hurt, actually hurt. There was a dull ache everywhere in her body.

Her eyes in the mirror were puffy and red. She must have been crying all night. She shivered. What was wrong with the furnace? She checked the thermostat. It was fine. There wasn't anything wrong with the heat. It was her. The coldness was inside her. She made a big pot of strong coffee and had something to eat. That made her feel a little better. She didn't even try to do any drawing.

Finally, she made a fire in the woodstove and tried to read. Every so often the words would get blurry. She wiped her eyes and found she was crying again. Damn. Damn Caldwell and Adam and the world full of men whom women cried over.

She must have dozed off, for when she awoke, the sun was streaming in the window, making golden puddles of light on the mellow pine floor.

She pulled on her boots and jacket and hat. For half an hour she shovelled snow as if her life depended on it. The strenuous work made her feel somewhat better.

Before the sun went down, the fellow who ploughed came up the hill and cleared the driveway. Tory looked out at the freshly cleared path of the drive. She was no longer snowed in. She could get out into the world of people if she wanted to. All she had to do was get in her car and drive down the hill. But she didn't. There wasn't any place she wanted to go, nor anyone she cared to see.

She popped some corn. That was always a happy thing to do. She associated popcorn with movies and friends and good times. But tonight the popcorn didn't work its magic. She ate a couple of handfuls and didn't want any more. She put the remainder out for the birds. She went to bed early. It had been a long day. Maybe she'd feel better tomorrow.

The following day she got up enough courage to go out into the woodshed. It was bare. Caldwell hadn't left a shred of paper. It was almost as though he had never been there.

She went back to her drawing-table, and was able to make a little progress on some sketches. It wasn't much, and she'd probably have to do them over. But it was a beginning.

When she went for groceries, she found herself looking at houses in the village. Was Caldwell in one of them? Where had he gone? She looked for his car, but didn't see it. It wasn't that she cared where he was, she told herself, she was just curious, that's all.

Several long days passed, and she was finally able to work again. There were still bouts of having to deal with eyes that cried all by themselves. She'd suddenly feel a great wave of sadness come over her, and her eyes would fill up and run over. She ruined one pen-and-ink drawing with big blotches of tears that made the ink run.

She was at her drawing-table when she heard a car pull up the drive. Her hand froze in mid-line.

Caldwell? Could it be? Who else would be calling on her?

She waited to hear the knock on the kitchen door before she got down from her stool.

She could hear children's voices on the other side of the door. That couldn't be Caldwell. She opened the door and found Sally standing on the stoep with Josh and Sara. 'My . . . hello!' She was so surprised, that she didn't know what to say.

'I had to come over the mountain to the dentist,' Sally explained. 'And we just thought we'd drop by and pay you a visit.'

'Come in . . . come in,' Tory replied. The children didn't wait to be asked twice. They swept by Tory into the kitchen.

'Where's Unca Mitch?' Sara asked, her eyes so like Mitchell's.

Tory gulped. Of course, they had come to see Mitchell. 'He's not here . . .' she began.

Sally touched her arm. 'I know. I'm sorry. I told Sara, but she's forgotten.' She smiled at Tory. 'I wanted to see you.'

'It wasn't working out . . .' Tory felt that she had to offer some explanation.

'I know,' Sally answered, 'Mitchell told us. I don't see why we can't still be friends though.' She looked a question at Tory.

'Of course,' Tory answered. 'I'd like that.'

'Good, then that's settled.'

Tory made hot chocolate, and they sat around the kitchen table and talked. It felt so good to talk to someone. Tory felt as though she had been away from civilisation for a very long time.

Little Sara put down her cup after taking a long sip. She had a chocolate moustache. She looked Tory straight in the eye: 'How come you live in Unca Mitch's house and he doesn't?'

'Because Unca Mitch doesn't live here any more,' Josh answered his sister.

'But Unca Mitch always lived here before,' Sara answered.

Josh didn't have an answer to that one. He looked at his mother for help.

'Your Unca Mitch was renting this house, he never owned it,' Sally explained. 'Tory bought the house. It's her house.'

'But this house is just about pretty near like our house,' Sara continued. 'I thought Unca Mitch was *supposed* to live here.'

You thought so too, didn't you? the little voice inside Tory's head insisted.

'No Sara, it doesn't work that way. I'll explain it to you later, okay?' Sally answered.

It was plain to see that Sara didn't want to leave it to be explained another time, but she agreed.

Sara finished her hot chocolate and started to leave the table, then she turned back and came to stand beside Tory. 'Don't you like Unca Mitch?' she asked, her pretty little face filled with concern.

'Of course she does,' Josh interjected. 'They're just friends, and friends don't live in each other's houses, that's all.'

Tory smiled in relief. Hurrah for Josh's logical, literal mind.

The children went out to play in the snow. 'I hope you'll excuse us . . . once again,' Sally smiled gently. 'My children seem to have a positive talent for asking embarrassing questions.'

'Don't worry,' Tory smiled. 'I don't mind. It's so interesting to see how their minds work, so direct.'

The two women were soon chatting like old friends. Caldwell had at least been right about one thing, Tory reflected. She and Sally were a lot alike.

'Alex is away this week,' Sally continued. 'He's attending a conference at Amherst. I'm so used to having him around, that I find it very lonely. Of course the children keep me company.'

'You're lucky to have them,' Tory answered.

'Say, I just had a brilliant idea,' Sally beamed. 'Why don't you come home with us for a couple of days? I would very much like to have you. It can't be too gay around here just now. Your being used to having someone around and all . . .'

'Well . . .' Tory began. She was tempted. She knew she needed to be with people.

'Come on,' Sally encouraged her. 'I have to come back to the dentist in two days. I can bring you back then. And in the meantime, we can keep each other company. It would be fun for me to have someone grown up to talk to.'

'All right,' Tory agreed. She could leave her work for two days. As a matter of fact, it would probably do her work good, to have her get away for two days.

Tory threw a few things in a suitcase. They were out of the door and headed down the drive before she had time to consider that she was going to spend two days with Mitchell Caldwell's sister and his niece and nephew. Which, now that she was thinking about it, might not be such a good idea. Well, it was too late now. They were on their way.

Sixteen

It was dark by the time they reached Sally's house. The children had fallen asleep in the car. Sally made soup for the children and put them to bed. Then she and Tory had a leisurely supper and talked until almost midnight.

'It's such a pleasure having you here,' Sally smiled. 'I'm so glad you decided to come.'

'It's a pleasure being here,' Tory answered. 'Thank you for asking me.' And she meant it. Being with Sally and the children made her feel half-way human again.

'I have to get up early and take Josh to school in the morning,' Sally went on. 'So if you get up and there's no one in the house, don't worry.'

They said good night, and Tory went directly to bed and slept soundly for the first time in many nights.

The house was quiet when she awoke in the morning. Sally must have taken Josh to school, she decided. Things were too quiet for the children to be in the house.

Tory got up and slipped into her robe, the one Mitchell had given her. She frowned. The warmth and softness of the cashmere made her catch her breath. She knew it wasn't the material, but the memory of the man who had given it to her. Maybe she should put it away, pack it in a box and put in on a shelf in her cupboard for a while . . . until she was well. How very similar getting over a love could be to getting over a sickness, Tory reflected.

She heard the door in the kitchen slam shut. Sally must be back. Tory ran a comb through her hair. How nice it was of Sally to have her. Sally was a very thoughtful person, not in the least like her brother.

Tory gave her hair one last swipe with the comb. She leaned forward to give herself a closer look in the mirror. The eyes weren't so puffy. She was beginning to look more normal, the effects of a lost love weren't so noticeable. The blue of the robe was very much the colour of her eyes, just as Caldwell had said. She shivered, and was very tempted to take off the robe right now. Yes, she would put it away when she got home. It wasn't the robe's fault that Caldwell had purchased it. Still, right now, she wasn't handling that fact too well.

Sally would be wondering if her houseguest was going to sleep all day. Tory headed for the kitchen, where she expected to find her hostess.

Tory was all the way into the kitchen before it became apparent that the person pouring a cup of coffee at the stove wasn't Sally. When the person turned to face her, Tory jumped a foot. It was Mitchell!

He was as surprised as she. 'What? Great Scott! What are you doing here?'

Even in the midst of her surprise, Tory noted that he looked a little peaked, as though he had been sick.

'I might ask you the same thing, Mr Caldwell!' The words came out like blocks of black ice.

'This is my sister's house,' Caldwell answered. 'What's your excuse? And where the devil is Sally?'

'Your sister very kindly invited me to visit her,' Tory continued in the same cold tones. 'She's gone to take Josh to school.'

Mitchell set the untasted cup of coffee on the table. 'If it's not too much trouble, Ms Higgins, please tell her I was here.' Then he turned on his heel and slammed out the door.

Tory stood there, as though she had turned to stone. Rude, rude, rude, she wanted to call after him. I love you, I love you, I love you, her mind also played over and over again. Tears rolled wet tracks down her cheeks. She heard the car in the drive. Still she stood in the same spot, undecided about what to do. She should go home, but Sally's appointment wasn't until tomorrow. Right now all she wanted in the world was to crawl into her own bed and pull the blankets over her head and forget everything for a while.

Tory couldn't believe her eyes. The kitchen

door opened and in came Mitchell, and behind him — Sally and Sara. The car she had heard hadn't been Mitchell leaving, but Sally arriving!

Tory wiped her face with the sleeve of her robe. Mitchell looked like thunder, and Sally didn't look much happier. Only little Sara seemed to take no notice of all the storms going on above her head in the world of grown ups. 'Can I have a banana, Mommy?'

'Yes,' Sally answered. 'Take it in the living-room. I think "Sesame Street" might be on TV just about now.'

Three pairs of stormy eyes watched the little girl walk over to the bowl of bananas and take her time choosing one. She beamed up at Sally. 'Thank you, Mommy.' Then she skipped out of the room.

Three voices began talking at once. 'Hold it!' Sally ordered. Mitchell and Tory fell silent. Sally looked daggers at them both. 'This is my house. You will grant me the privilege of speaking first.' She looked from one to the other. 'I have never seen such stubborn people in all my life. Now, it's obvious that you two need to talk . . . to each other. So talk!' She folded her arms and waited.

'This isn't going to work . . .' Mitchell began.

'None of that!' Sally ordered. 'You talk to each other.'

She waited. The room filled up with silence. They could hear gay chatty voices coming from the TV in the living-room. The silence lengthened. Finally Sally could stand it no more. 'All right,' she began, 'if you two won't talk, then I will.' She cleared her throat. 'It's plain to see that the two of you love each other . . .'

Mitchell and Tory both began to talk at once.

'Silence!' Sally ordered. 'Sit down!' For some reason they both did as she ordered, although it was plain to see that neither wanted to.

'I gave you your chance to speak, and you didn't take it. Now, it's my turn.' She looked first at one and then the other. 'As I was saying, you love each other. You don't have to bother denying it, I could see it very clearly, when you were here at Thanksgiving. Even the children saw it.' She glared at them both, daring them to contradict her. 'Now, that's settled. What remains to be done, is for you both to talk. There's nothing that can't be settled between two people who love each other. I know what I'm talking about. Alex and I have a very good marriage. It works well for both of us,' she smiled. 'And it works well because we talk to each other! None of this silent-treatment rot. Why do you suppose we encourage our children to speak their minds? We want them to be happy. We want them to have good communicating skills. We want them to have good marriages.' She paused and sat back in her chair. 'There, I've said enough. You don't need a sermon; you need to talk! I'm going to go into the living-room and watch "Sesame Street" with my daughter. And you two are going to sit right here and talk until you have everything settled between you.'

Sally got up and poured herself a cup of coffee. 'Help yourselves to coffee if you want.' Then she left the room.

Mitchell was studying his hands, folded in front of him on the table. Tory was slumped down in her chair, contemplating the space before her.

'Want some coffee?' he asked.

Tory nodded her head.

Mitchell poured two cups and handed her one. 'Well, what do you think?' he asked.

'I think she's right,' Tory answered, 'we should talk.'

'Good,' Mitchell replied. 'Do you want me to begin?'

Tory nodded.

Mitchell took a long sip of his coffee. His strong hands on the coffee-cup made Tory's insides squirm. Could it be that he loved her? He hadn't denied it.

'I have been labouring under the impression that you are, shall we say, a thoroughly modern woman, who doesn't need a permanent relationship in her life. Is that true?'

Tory sat up straighter. 'Yes . . . no . . . I mean, well I guess I thought so, or wanted to think so.'

Mitchell raised his eyebrows. 'Would you care to clarify that? That has to be the longest "maybe" I've ever heard.' Just the smallest amount of grin played around the corners of his mouth.

'There was once a man in my life,' Tory began,

'who became the centre of my life. I wrapped all my dreams around him. He left. That's when I decided that permanent relationships were dangerous to one's health and well-being.'

'I see,' Mitchell frowned.

'I thought I could live a nicely adequate life on my own . . . until you came along. I thought I could be, as you say, thoroughly modern, but my heart wasn't having any of that. It wouldn't let me do it that way.' Tory paused.

'Go on.'

'And since you said you weren't interested in any permanent relationship now, or maybe ever, I . . . well, I just thought . . .' Her voice trailed off. She frowned.

'Yes?'

'When I went down to New York for Andy's wedding, she told me I should tell you I loved you. I was sincerely considering it . . . until I called and that Lisa person answered my phone! That's when I decided I was again being a fool about love. That's when I decided that I had to throw you out of my life . . . before you threw me out of yours.'

She was crying again. Caldwell didn't touch her. She wanted him to reach across the table and pat her hand. She wanted him to come around and take her in his arms. He didn't. She was making a fool of herself. It didn't matter. She needed to tell him, wanted to tell him the whole story. Then, they could each go their own way. At least she would have had her say. Maybe it would make her feel better.

Mitchell was silent for a long while. 'You're right,' he said at last. 'I did say I wasn't interested in a permanent relationship. I thought I wasn't. You'll also remember I said I had just come through a messy divorce. I had been married to a woman who took me for every cent I had. She wasn't interested in me, or in having my children. She liked the kind of life I could provide for her. It took me a long time to get it through my thick head that she didn't love me. Probably she wasn't capable of loving anyone but herself. Anyway, I wasn't ever going to put myself in that position again. Our stories aren't too much different, are they?'

Tory shook her head. She didn't trust her voice to answer him.

'As far as that person Lisa is concerned,' he smiled at her, 'she's just a friend who stopped by. I asked her if she'd telephone-sit while I ran to the store. I was afraid you'd call while I was out, which is exactly what you did. If Lisa was rude to you, I'm sorry. But that's just Lisa. She enjoys stirring things up. I wouldn't get involved with Lisa with a ten-foot pole. I've had enough stir-up to last seven lifetimes. I could have told you all this, but you didn't give me a chance to explain.' He was smiling at her now.

'I'm truly sorry,' she answered. 'I was so hurt and angry, I wasn't thinking straight.'

'You know, my dear landlady, I think I began to fall in love with you the first time you stepped into my . . . I mean, your kitchen.'

'You love me?' Tory asked. She was having a hard time believing her ears.

'Of course. Isn't it obvious?' He was grinning at her, warmly, invitingly. 'I made up my mind that first day that I was going to move in with you and make you love me too.'

'You're kidding?'

'Nope. And then, there was the part of me that was scared to death too.'

'Sounds just like me.'

'Yep.' He scraped back his chair and went to the stove to pour himself another cup of coffee. 'More?' He held up the coffee pot.

Tory looked at her cup. She hadn't taken a sip of her first cup yet. 'No, thank you.' Mitchell loved her! Mitchell Caldwell loved her! Imagine that!

Mitchell sipped his coffee. 'Now, isn't there something more that you want to tell me?'

'More? What more?'

'Oh, like I love you, too, Mitchell,' he answered casually.

'I love you too,' she answered. She got up and floated around to where he was standing, love shining out of his eyes, blazing at her. He put down his cup and gently took her in his arms. 'Oh, Mitchell, I do love you so.'

'And I you,' he whispered, then he kissed her. It seemed to Tory that she melted into his lips. If Mitchell's strong arms hadn't been around her, she probably would have dissolved on to the floor.

When they finally came up for air, Mitchell smoothed back her hair. 'To think we almost lost everything.' He shook his head.

'We were both a couple of fools,' Tory agreed.

'Just another way that we're alike.' Mitchell pulled her body even closer to his, and rocked her in his arms. 'Oh Tory, Victoria, my love,' he crooned in her ear.

She turned her face up to look at him. 'Promise me one thing.'

'Anything, my darling girl.'

'Promise me you won't ever leave again, no matter what I say.'

'You have my word.' He tipped her chin up so that he could kiss her lips again.

The sound of laughter coming from the living-room made them remember where they were. 'Whew, it's a good thing they laughed just now,' he grinned at her. 'Otherwise, I would have made love to you right here, right now.'

Tory smiled. She could feel the hardness of his desire for her against her body. He was right, she would have happily let him. 'Mitchell?' she asked. 'Shall we go home?'

'Gladly. Eagerly. Right now. Hurry, my love.' He playfully smacked her bottom, as she pulled away to gather her belongings and to get dressed.

Tory threw on her clothes with shaking fingers. She had to rebutton her blouse twice. In her haste she kept getting it wrong.

Sally's eyes were shining as she wished them goodbye.

Mitchell looked at his sister through narrowed eyes. 'You set us up, didn't you?'

Sally nodded happily. 'I knew if I got you two together that things would just naturally work out. Simple.' She shrugged her shoulders.

Tory gave Sally a hug. 'Thank you, thank you. I don't know how to thank you.'

'Just be happy, that's all,' Sally answered warmly.

'You can count on it,' Mitchell replied. 'We intend to do just that!'

They could barely wait to get home. Tory's whole body ached for Mitchell. She reached over and rubbed his thighs, as they sped through the mountains. 'Oh,' he moaned. 'That feels so good . . . but you'd better not do that. I'll have us up a tree. With your delicious body so near to me, it's all I can do to keep my eyes on the road.'

They even considered stopping somewhere beside the road, but the country was high with snow banks. 'If it were summer,' Mitchell grinned, 'we wouldn't get home for weeks . . . if then.'

'Oh?' Tory asked.

'I'd have to stop every five minutes to roll in the grass for another taste of you,' he replied.

'Yum,' Tory laughed delightedly. 'I can hardly wait.'

Finally, the car rolled up the driveway. The sun was bright on the cosy little house. It had never looked so much like home.

They rushed into the house, not even bothering to bring Tory's luggage in with them. They peeled off jackets and coats and hats as they went. When they got to the bedroom, they laughed and giggled as they peeled off each other's clothes. Mitchell ran his hands up and down Tory's soft smooth skin. Tory's eyes were wide in astonishment. She would never have believed that this could happen to her. Mitchell picked her up and put her on the bed, then he lay down beside her. 'I don't know where to start. I want to kiss your lips, your toes, the tip of your nose.'

Tory's wild hands were rubbing him, kneading his back. 'Start here,' she whispered, her voice heavy with passion. She kissed him on the lips.

He ran his tongue around her lips, then inside her waiting mouth. And all the while, his hands were busy caressing every inch of her quaking skin.

'I can see these need immediate attention.' He fell on her erect nipples with hot kisses. His nips sent spasms of pleasure all through her body. His kisses trailed down her belly.

Tory took his throbbing manhood in her hand. She guided it to the seat of her hot desire. There was nothing between them. Their bodies were together as one, swaying, moving, the rhythm of their passion flowing strong, as a river in spring flood, through their veins. On and on they went. They were being swept away, down the swollen river. Deeper and deeper into the current they flowed, the waters of passion driving them onward. They arched for a second over the falls. And then they were falling, melting as one into the waters of passion spent. Slowly Tory felt life return to her tempest-tossed body. Never before had Tory felt so complete, so empty, and yet so whole. The power of love was beyond description, beyond feeling.

Mitchell lay beside her on the bed, his face buried in her hair. He kissed her gently on the ear. 'Will you marry me, Ms Landlady?'

'On one condition,' Tory answered.

'What's that?'

'That you stop calling me landlady.'

'How does Mrs Caldwell sound to you?'

'Splendid!' she answered.

They slept, and made love and talked, and then did it all again.

We hope you have enjoyed this Large Print book. Other G.K. Hall & Co. or Chivers Press Large Print books are available at your library or directly from the publishers.

For more information about current and upcoming titles, please call or write, without obligation, to:

G.K. Hall & Co.
P.O. Box 159
Thorndike, Maine 04986 USA
Tel. (800) 223-1244

OR

Chivers Press Limited
Windsor Bridge Road
Bath BA2 3AX
England
Tel. (0225) 335336

All our Large Print titles are designed for easy reading, and all our books are made to last.

Shadow Tag

ALSO BY LOUISE ERDRICH

Novels

Love Medicine
The Beet Queen
Tracks
The Crown of Columbus (*with Michael Dorris*)
The Bingo Palace
Tales of Burning Love
The Antelope Wife
The Last Report on the Miracles at Little No Horse
The Master Butchers Singing Club
Four Souls
The Painted Drum
The Plague of Doves

Stories

The Red Convertible: New and Selected Stories, 1978–2008

Poetry

Jacklight
Baptism of Desire
Original Fire

For Children

Grandmother's Pigeon
The Birchbark House
The Range Eternal
The Game of Silence
The Porcupine Year

Nonfiction

The Blue Jay's Dance
Books and Islands in Ojibwe Country